# PEA'S BOOK
## OF HOLIDAYS

www.randomhousechildrens.co.uk

# PEA'S BOOK
### OF
# HOLIDAYS

## SUSIE DAY

RED FOX

PEA'S BOOK OF HOLIDAYS
A RED FOX BOOK 978 1 782 95260 2

First published in Great Britain by Red Fox Books,
an imprint of Random House Children's Publishers UK
A Random House Group Company

This edition published 2014

1 3 5 7 9 10 8 6 4 2

The Random House Group Limited supports the Forest Stewardship Council® (FSC®),
the leading international forest-certification organisation. Our books carrying the FSC
label are printed on FSC®-certified paper. FSC is the only forest-certification scheme
supported by the leading environmental organisations, including Greenpeace. Our paper
procurement policy can be found at www.randomhouse.co.uk/environment

MIX
Paper from
responsible sources
FSC® C016897

Set in 13/18pt Baskerville MT by Falcon Oast Graphic Art

Red Fox Books are published by Random House Children's Publishers UK,
61–63 Uxbridge Road, London W5 5SA

www.**randomhousechildrens**.co.uk
www.**totallyrandombooks**.co.uk
www.**randomhouse**.co.uk

Addresses for companies within The Random House Group Limited can be found at:
www.randomhouse.co.uk/offices.htm

THE RANDOM HOUSE GROUP Limited Reg. No. 954009

A CIP catalogue record for this book is available from the British Library.

Printed and bound in Great Britain by
CPI Group (UK) Ltd, Croydon CR0 4YY

For Rachel and Matthew

# CHAPTER 1

# GOODBYE, CLOVER

Pea stood at the foot of the stairs, and stared at the clock.

It was forty-nine minutes and fifty-four seconds past nine, on the very first day of the school holidays.

Fifty-five seconds past nine.

Fifty-six.

*Tick, tick, tick.*

Pea took a deep breath.

'Ten-minute warning!' yelled Tinkerbell, speeding out of the kitchen, a damp and drippy

Wuffly at her heels. They leaped up the stairs two at a time. 'Clover! Mum! *Ten-minute warning!*'

There was a wail of horror from Clover's bedroom.

'I'm still in my dressing gown! I can't go to theatre camp in my dressing gown!'

'Then you should probably get dressed, flower,' called Mum from the bathroom.

'And I haven't got socks!'

'You have hundreds of socks, flower.'

'Only grey bobbly ones – not good ones for showing off to important actor people.'

'Even important actor people wear grey bobbly socks, my lamb.'

'Argh – wet dog in my suitcase! Shoo, Wuffly! No, don't chew that. Help, Tink. *Help!*'

Wuffly bounded back down the stairs, Clover's Best for Blondes shampoo bottle clutched triumphantly in her jaws.

'I'm getting it!' yelled Tinkerbell, chasing Wuffly's wet tail past Pea and back into the kitchen.

'That was *my* job,' said Pea softly, to the clock. '*I* was doing the ten-minute warning.'

The kitchen door banged shut. There was a scuffle, a yelp, then silence. Upstairs fell silent too. All Pea could hear was the sound of the rain, tapping at their raspberry-red front door.

The Llewellyn house was not often so peaceful. Once upon a time the family had travelled all over the world and lived in all sorts of exotic locations – Madagascar, Norway, Prestatyn – but now they lived in Kensal Rise, north London. They did try to be sensible, mostly. But Clover (who was fourteen, with a sweet pink face and tumbling blonde hair like Mum's) liked to sing show tunes in the bath, and in the garden, and in bed. Tinkerbell (who was eight, with brown skin and tight black curls like her father) liked explosions and hitting things with hammers – which meant Mum did quite a lot of shouting. The fact that Pea (who was twelve, with violently red hair) spent a lot of time reading books and writing stories in her little attic

**3**

bedroom – quietly, without bothering anyone – hardly mattered.

Fortunately the Llewellyns had very kind next-door neighbours, the Paget-Skidelskys, who didn't mind singing or explosions, and sometimes shouted at their children too.

But now the summer holidays were here at last, it was all change.

In ten minutes' time – more like eight, now – Clover would go off in a taxi to Cheseman Hall theatre camp for the whole school holidays. There would be classes on voice projection, singing, even sword-fighting.

The next day, Pea and Tinkerbell would be whisked away too – by Tinkerbell's dad, Clem: first for two weeks of camping in the Lake District, then back to Clem's new flat in Tenby until the end of August.

Meanwhile Mum would stay at home in London, all alone, to finish writing her book.

Mum was simply Mum at home, but the rest

of the world knew her as Marina Cove, super-star author of the *Mermaid Girls* books. Now she was beginning a whole new series called *Pirate Girls* – although, to Pea's relief, the ghostly mermaid Coraly (who had bright red hair just like hers)would be in the new stories too. Mum had already been locked away in her study for weeks, but the first *Pirate Girls* book had to be finished by the end of the holidays, or Nozomi Handa, Mum's Dreaded Editor, would be very angry.

The Llewellyn girls would be separated for the summer. For the first time ever, Pea would be the older sister, not the middlest. The big girl. The boss. The one who absolutely, definitely had to be listened to, all summer.

She was looking forward to it rather a lot.

Pea looked up at the clock. *Seven minutes to go.*

The kitchen door creaked open, and a forlorn Tinkerbell peered out.

'Pea. Help?' she whispered.

Behind her, Pea could see a crushed shampoo bottle oozing lemon-scented goo across the kitchen floor – and an even more forlorn Wuffly, tail drooping, hairy grey jaws covered in froth.

Pea sighed. Perhaps being the oldest wouldn't make that much difference: Tinkerbell would still be Tinkerbell.

Wuffly tried to lick the bubbles off, then sneezed, whined, and sneezed again. Bubbles frothed out of her nose. She whimpered, her paws doing an unhappy jerky dance across the floor – into the puddle of goo, which made her skid and slide and froth even more.

'All right – it's OK, don't panic,' said Pea as Tinkerbell's eyes grew very wide.

Pea sent them both out into the back garden to defrothify in the rain, while she cleaned up the goo with kitchen paper. The Best for Blondes bottle went in the bin.

Suddenly the house rang out with noise: three

alarm clocks, her own beepy digital watch, and the chorus of 'Part of Your World' from *The Little Mermaid* from Mum's mobile phone.

'Five-minute warning!' Pea shouted, running for the stairs.

'It's fine, I'm ready, I'm completely ready!'

There was a series of thumps and bumps. Clover arrived at the bottom of the stairs, pink-cheeked and beaming, a fat blue suitcase at her feet. 'See? Nearly five minutes early. I told you there was no need for all the fuss.'

The fat blue suitcase creaked. Then it burst open, like two halves of a clam. Out spilled hairbands, cotton balls, and an enormous quantity of socks.

'Clover!' Mum hurried down the stairs behind her, and stared in horror at the exploded case. 'I thought you were taking the wheelie case we borrowed from next door?'

'I like yours better,' said Clover, shovelling socks back inside. 'It's vintagey. Old blue suitcases

**7**

are much more actor-ish than zippy ones with wheels.'

'Not if you can't fit half your things in them, they aren't. Although . . . why do you need this, exactly? Or these?'

Mum held up a top hat, a pair of oversized spectacles with no glass in the frames, and a collection of stick-on moustaches.

'In case we decide to put on a show and need to improvise costumes!' said Clover. 'Cheseman Hall theatre camp encourages its students to follow their own creative pathways – it said so in the brochure. It's an actor thing, Mum. You wouldn't understand.'

'I suppose that explains why my best blue skirt is in here too, hmm? Well, that reduces the pile by one, at least. Hang on – where's your raincoat? Have you packed *any* warm clothes? Come on, my pumpkin. Even actors have to be a tiny bit sensible.'

Pea knelt down beside Clover, and helped

**8**

her sort the spilled packing into three piles: necessary (knickers, mobile phone for emergencies, her notepaper with tiny blue forget-me-nots round the edges); maybes (Mum allowed the moustaches, but not the top hat); and definite nos.

'Oh, *Clover*!' said Mum.

At the very bottom of the case was a large photograph in a pale wooden frame of them all gathered around last year's Christmas tree. Mum was halfway through eating a mince pie. Pea had her eyes shut. Tinkerbell was mostly obscured by a blur of hairy grey dog. But it was a beautiful picture of Clover: perfectly posed, with sparkly eyes and a warm smile.

The real Clover had the grace to look slightly ashamed. 'I know,' she said, clutching the photo to her chest. 'Sorry. But it's the nicest one I've got of me – and I couldn't go away all summer without a picture of you all to put on my bedside table, to say goodnight to. Look, it's even got Clem in it.'

She held out the picture, and pointed at the reflection in the mirror on the wall behind the Christmas tree. If you squinted, you could just make out Clem's elbow.

Pea felt guilty. She'd already started a packing list of essentials for their camping trip.

**THINGS TO TAKE ON HOLIDAY**
Books
My owl notebook
My Special Writing Pen
Spare not-special pen
Emergency biscuits
CDs for the car (or Clem will play his Oasis
    CD and do singing/chair-dancing)
Tent

She made a mental note to add a photo of Mum and Clover to say goodnight to.

Mum gave Clover a kiss on the nose. 'That's sweet, my petal.' She slipped the picture out of the heavy frame and tucked it back into the case.

There was a loud honking from a taxi in the street outside.

'No-minutes warning!' yelled Tinkerbell, racing back in from the garden, soaked to the skin, as a sopping Wuffly bounded down the hallway to bark at the noise. 'Off you go to Cheese Camp!'

'It's Cheseman Hall *theatre* camp, not *Cheese* Camp,' said Clover hotly.

The taxi honked again.

Pea looked up at the clock with a pang.

Ten o'clock exactly.

It was time to say goodbye for the whole summer.

Since she was already wet, Tinkerbell was sent out into the rain to tell the taxi to wait.

Clover flung on as many of the spilled clothes as she could fit over what she was already wearing – three jumpers and a pair of stripy leggings doubling up as a quirky scarf – and the rest were shovelled back into the suitcase. She sat on it until it clicked shut.

Pea fetched brown parcel tape from the study, and they looped it around the case three times, just to make sure.

'Will that do?' asked Mum.

Clover smiled. 'It looks more actor-ish than ever,' she said happily. 'Oh, I'm so excited! I'm going to learn so many things – tap dancing, and how to sound like a Cockney urchin – and I'm going to meet the most amazing people . . . But I promise I'll write, and phone, and in the bits when I'm not too busy actor-ing, I expect I'll miss you terribly. Give my love to Clem, and enjoy your camping, and good luck with the new book— Oh, he's honking again, I'd better go!'

There were goodbye hugs; very tight ones.

Then Clover was dragging the fat blue suitcase out into the rain and along the crazy paving.

'Umbrella?' shouted Mum.

'Um. I think it ended up inside the suitcase,' said Pea.

Mum picked up the top hat, ran after Clover, and plonked it on her head. 'Go on, take it. It'll keep the rain off, at least.'

With a swish of windscreen wipers and a flurry of waves, Clover was gone.

Pea, Tinkerbell and Wuffly lingered on the doorstep, watching the raindrops.

'Did you tell her about the shampoo?' whispered Tinkerbell.

Pea shook her head.

Tinkerbell shrugged. 'Oh well. I expect dirty hair is actor-ish too.'

# CHAPTER
# 2

# A YELLOW
# TENT

Pea lay flat on her sleeping bag, and listened to the rain thrumming on the roof of the tent.

'What *are* you two doing out there?' shouted Mum from safe inside the house.

'Camping practice,' Tinkerbell shouted back. 'We're pretending to be outdoors holiday people, in the countryside. Go away – you're spoiling it.'

The tent was big and yellow, not quite tall enough to stand up in, with a new plasticky smell. Pea's friend Molly's mum had lent it to them, with a confession that she'd never actually taken it out of

14

its bag – so to check there were no missing poles or pegs, Pea and Tinkerbell had put it up in the back garden last night.

It had begun to rain the moment the last peg had slid into the lawn, and hadn't stopped since.

'At least it's definitely waterproof,' said Pea, prodding the groundsheet to check for leaky holes.

'Mm,' said Tinkerbell, her nose in her book.

'Noisy, though.'

'Mm,' said Tinkerbell.

'It'd be more comfy with pillows – underneath us, like a bed.'

'No!' Tinkerbell put her book down crossly, and rolled over to lie on her front and glare at Pea. 'That's cheating. It has to be mattresses made from heather covered by a rug, or we're not doing it properly.'

Pea nodded solemnly, suppressing a smile.

Pea herself had always been the reader in the family. Tinkerbell didn't mind fact books with pictures of spiders, or instructions for how to make an indoor volcano, but she was usually too busy plotting her own villainous schemes to bother with made-up ones in stories. Back in June, however, Tinkerbell had been laid up in bed with a week-long sicky bug, of the sort that makes the whole house smell queasy and chicken soupish. Pea had tried to cheer her up with a pile of comforting books from the library – audio ones, on CD, since she was too sicky to read for herself.

Tinkerbell had played Enid Blyton's *Five on a Treasure Island* over and over until the whole family could recite great chunks of it, from hearing it float across the landing.

Ever since, Tinkerbell would come home from their Saturday morning library trip with armfuls of Blyton: *Secret Seven*s and *Five Find-Outer*s, but especially *Famous Five*s. The Famous Five solved mysteries, usually by doing dangerous things in caves or boats. They had a dog. They ate a gigantic amount of food, and no one ever told them off for being spectacularly rude – which they were, quite often. It was like Tinkerbell's dream life, in a book.

Pea had never been all that keen on pictures of spiders, or villainous schemes. She herself preferred the school stories Enid Blyton had written – *Malory Towers*, and *St Clare's* – but she'd loved the *Famous Five* books too. It was nice, having a thing they shared.

So when Clem had asked what sort of holiday they might like to go on together, the answer was obvious. (Tinkerbell at first requested a castle with dungeons full of smuggled treasure, but it had been agreed that camping was sufficiently Famous Five-ish, and a lot easier to book on the internet.)

Two weeks of camping, and all the mystery-solving adventures they could muster.

'Go on – add heather and rugs to the packing list,' said Tinkerbell, nose back in *Five Run Away Together*. 'We should take some with us, in case they don't have any in the Lake District.'

Pea wasn't sure they had any in Kensal Rise,

either. In fact, she thought having a yellow plasticky-smelling waterproof tent meant they might already be cheating enough for a pillow or two not to matter – but it didn't seem worth arguing.

**MORE THINGS TO TAKE ON HOLIDAY**
Heather and rugs
Swimming things
Ginger beer-bottle opener
Small pan for boiling eggs
Torch
Spare batteries
Stub of pencil (for drawing treasure maps)
Rope (for climbing into smugglers' caves)
Family photo (one where everyone looks
   nice)

There was a bang outside as the back door of the house swung open again.

'Are you cold, my chicks?' called Mum. 'I could bring you woolly jumpers? Or hot chocolate?'

'No!' shouted Tinkerbell, unzipping the tent just enough to poke her head out into the rain. 'Stop bothering us! Leave us alone to practise being proper campers!' She zipped the zip shut again, and folded her arms crossly.

'That was rude,' said Pea.

Tinkerbell's pout got bigger.

'We are going off on holiday and leaving her all by herself, Tink.'

'We haven't even gone yet!'

'I know. But I think she might be doing some missing us in advance.'

'That's stupid. She could come on holiday too, if she wanted.'

'Not really. Not even if she didn't have a book to finish.'

Mum and Clem were still friendly – not always cross with each other like Pea's friend Molly's parents were – but they hadn't lived together for a very long time. Ever since they'd moved to London, Clem had come to visit and do Dad-like things – with all of them, not just Tinkerbell. (Clover's dad had died when she was a baby, and Pea had never met hers: she'd tried to track him down not long ago, but he remained a sort of mystery – and not the kind it might be fun for the Famous Five to solve.)

But still, it wasn't like having a mum and a dad who did all their family things together. Mum did the parent-stuff, like bedtimes, and making sure their plates had vegetables on, and hugs when they were sad. Clem was more of a fun person who popped up at special moments, and birthdays. Like Father Christmas, but more often. And more Jamaican. And he didn't always bring presents.

Having a whole summer with just him looking after them was like a special treat. And Mum wasn't invited. Pea could see why she might feel a bit left out.

'You know, I would quite like a hot chocolate,' said Pea casually.

Tinkerbell nodded.

Pea unzipped the tent just enough to stick her head out into the rain. 'Mum? If we're sorry for being horrible, can we have hot chocolate after all?'

After a bit of nudging, Tinkerbell stuck her head out too. 'If you aren't very busy, you could come out here and help us practise camping as well. If you promise to have a small bottom, because the tent is quite full of books and us already.'

Mum reappeared at the kitchen door, and gave them a thumbs-up and a grin. A moment later, they heard the swirly sound of water filling up the kettle.

Pea zipped them back in, and bundled herself up in her sleeping bag, shaking raindrops out of her eyes. 'Do you think Clem knows about bedtimes? And having to eat your sandwiches before the chocolate biscuit in your packed lunch?'

'Probably not,' said Tinkerbell gleefully. 'Let's not tell him.'

But as it turned out, they wouldn't need to.

'Quick, quick – come inside, my ducks!' Mum called from the back door. 'Clem's on Skype, and he says he needs to talk to you both!'

They scrambled out of their sleeping bags and dashed through the rain back into the house.

In the study, Mum's old computer was on, with Clem's big pixelly face filling the screen. He looked awfully tired, Pea thought. His eyes were red. There were grey tufts in his curly black hair, and instead of his usual cosy jumper, he was wearing some sort of pastel-coloured top with what looked like a ribbon round the neck.

'There's my girls,' he said, smiling weakly. 'How are you doing, babes?'

Tinkerbell gave the screen a wave. 'We're brilliant, Dad – we've put the tent up so we know how to do it – there's three poles and they spring together with elastic bits, and me and Pea did it all by ourselves without even any help, and we've checked it's waterproof, and I'm going to

**22**

build a campfire – not yet, Mum, when we go, don't worry – and I've read twenty-three pages of my *Famous Five* book just this morning, and I'm going to bring ten books or maybe more, and if I run out I'll read Pea's, and do you know if they have heather and rugs in the Lake District? Because if not, we'll bring some.'

Clem laughed, then coughed, the sound coming out strange and bubbly through the computer speakers.

'Steady on, Stinks, yeah? That all sounds amazing. But I've got news, girls. Bad news. I'm so sorry about this, but . . . we can't go. I can't take you camping. I'm in hospital. The holiday's off.'

# CHAPTER
# 3

# MORE BAD NEWS

'What?' said Mum.

'Where?' said Pea.

'*Why?*' wailed Tinkerbell.

On the computer screen, Clem's face froze for a moment – lips parted, eyebrows crunched together in confusion. Then he came back to life, halfway through a sentence.

'. . . thought it was just a cold, like, but the cough wouldn't go, and then my back started to hurt, and . . .'

The screen froze again.

'. . . double pneumonia, apparently. I'm on a drip, antibiotics, the works.'

'You're in hospital right now?' asked Pea.

Clem nodded, coughing again.

'But . . . what about our holiday?' said Tinkerbell.

Pea was wondering the same thing – but she could see Mum in the corner of the screen, giving Tinkerbell a severe look.

'Shush, Tink. Clem, what do the doctors say?' Mum asked in a gentle voice. 'Are you going to be all right?'

Pea stiffened. Was pneumonia the very bad sort of ill? Could it be?

Clem rubbed his eyes with his thumbs. There was a lump of plastic sticking out of the back of his hand, with a tube going into it. It made Pea feel vaguely sick, so she looked at the tip of his left ear instead.

'They reckon I'll be in here for two weeks – could be longer. Then bed rest after that. Basically, I'm out for the whole summer.'

Tinkerbell made a gulping noise, and ran out of the room.

Mum hurried after her.

Pea was left alone with Clem's big face, and the horrible tube sticking out of his hand. He looked terribly ill, suddenly. It was hard not to keep thinking about the tube, even while staring at his ear.

'Um. I'm very sorry you're poorly,' she whispered eventually. 'Can we . . . should we come to visit? To help look after you, I mean? I know we couldn't stay at the hospital, but we could go back and forth on the train. Or maybe me and Tink could stay in a hotel till you're feeling a bit better . . . We could use the money Granny Duff left us.'

Clover's Granny Duff had died a few months before, and left them each a small inheritance. It had paid for Clover's summer at Cheseman Hall. Mum had put Pea's and Tinkerbell's shares in the bank, to be saved for 'something important'. This sounded exactly that.

But Clem was shaking his head slowly. 'Babes, that's really kind, but . . . I'm pretty sick, love. I'm not up to having you two rampaging about the place.'

'We wouldn't rampage,' said Pea. 'I'm not sure I even know how.'

Clem sighed. 'Best thing you can do for me, Pea, is be a big sensible girl and look after your little sister, yeah? Make sure she still has a fun summer. That's what'll make me feel better. OK?'

Pea thought about all the time she'd spent looking forward to being the eldest, now that Clover was away. This wasn't what she'd imagined at all. But she stood up very straight, and nodded.

Mum led a tear-stained Tinkerbell back into the study.

'We'll go camping next summer, love,' said

Clem, his voice sounding hoarse. 'Or at half term, maybe. We'll camp next time, I promise. Proper promise. You'll still have a good time – right, Pea?' He managed a wink.

They blew him kisses, and made heart-shapes with their hands. Then the screen went blank.

'This is the worst holiday ever,' sniffed Tinkerbell, wrapping her arms around Wuffly's neck.

'Poor Clem,' said Mum.

'Poor *us*,' said Tinkerbell.

Pea wasn't sure it was allowed to feel sad for themselves, when Clem was so very poorly – but she did all the same.

No camping. No Clem. No holiday at all.

Pea sat in the tent and listened to the rain hammering down.

'We can still *read* about going camping,' she said, trying to sound bright as she prodded the pile of library books stacked at the back.

Tinkerbell lifted her head, just enough for Pea to see one brown eye glaring at her in disgust.

'Look, you haven't started this one yet – *Five Have a Wonderful Time*.'

'That's a stupid name for a book,' sulked Tinkerbell, kicking it. 'I don't want to read about people having a wonderful time. I want to read *Five Build an Explosive Device*, or *Five Set Fire to Stupid Pneumonia with Laser Beams from Their Eyes*.'

'Well, you can't!' said Pea crossly, snatching up the book before Tinkerbell could kick it again. 'Enid Blyton didn't write those sorts of stories.'

'Well, she *should* have!' Tinkerbell buried her face in her sleeping bag, her fists clenched tight.

If Clem was here, Pea thought, he'd know just what to say to make Tinkerbell giggle and forget all about why she was sad. But if he was here, then she wouldn't *be* sad.

When she was miserable, Pea usually wrote something, to distract herself. (Currently she was working on *The Adventures of Black-Eyed Pea*, about a Robin Hood-ish pirate who only robbed from other pirates, and gave their plundered treasure to unfortunate sailors with small shabby boats and unshiny buttons.)

'Why don't you write them, then?' she said slowly. 'I bet Clem would like something to read in hospital. He'll probably be really bored without us.'

Tinkerbell's fists unclenched. 'A whole book?' she said, eyeing Pea with suspicion.

'A short one. I'll lend you my owl notebook. And my Special Writing Pen.'

(Pea's Special Writing Pen wrote in purple ink, and had a tiny floating owl inside which flew back and forth when tilted.)

Tinkerbell sat up with a smile. Moments later, she was hard at work.

Pea wrapped her sleeping bag around her, and opened the *Famous Five* book. She was too old for it really, but at that moment she very much wanted to read about people having a wonderful time, with children who got to go on exactly the holidays they liked, and no one had pneumonia.

Soon she was lost to a comforting world of missing scientists, and sinister faces at castle windows.

'How do you spell *decapitated*?' asked Tinkerbell.

'Why?'

Tinkerbell thrust the notebook under Pea's nose.

Five Go on a Boat That Sinks
Five Get Lost in a Monster Jungle and
   One of Them Gets Savagely Eaten by
   Lions
Four (Because One of Them Got Eaten)
   Get Sent to Prison Even Though They
   Didn't Do It and Then Escape with Guns
Five Get D

'I thought I'd start with titles, and then write the insides of whichever one sounds best.'

There was a sudden outbreak of barking from inside the house: Wuffly, and the familiar yapping of the rather wild puppy from the house next door.

'Hooray!' yelled Tinkerbell. 'The Sams must be here. I'm going to get Sam One to draw my book cover for me. He's good at monsters and people being eaten.'

Their neighbours, the Paget-Skidelskys, were two mums, two Sams (ten-year-old twins, a boy and a girl), and Surprise, the little dog.

Sam One was indeed good at drawing – and he would be good at saying something calming and cheerful about cancelled holidays too. Sam Two was occasionally mean, and always slightly dangerous – but Tinkerbell liked that. Pea felt better at once. They could be the Famous Five together: four children and a dog, plus an extra dog for spare. They didn't need to go on holiday.

They could find a mystery to solve together, right here in London.

Filled with hope, Pea tucked in her bookmark and hurried after Tinkerbell into the kitchen . . . but it was not to be.

'We've come to say goodbye!' said Dr Paget, resting her hands on the twins' shoulders while Mum frantically chased the dogs around the kitchen table. 'I'm whisking the twins off to Norfolk to visit their cousins.'

'For a whole fortnight!' said Dr Skidelsky, with some glee.

'Really?' said Pea.

The two Sams nodded.

'We're going to go horse-riding,' said Sam Two smugly.

'Probably,' said Sam One, looking nervous.

Tinkerbell made a small noise of despair.

'We brought cake,' said Dr Paget, giving Dr Skidelsky an urgent nudge.

Dr Skidelsky produced a tin containing a

thick round fruit cake studded with red cherries.

'Well – um – that's very kind, isn't it, my lambs?' said Mum breathlessly. 'That'll be lovely with a cup of tea. Tink, Sam, sort these ridiculous dogs out, will you? Sam – yes, you – cups are in that cupboard. Pea, shift all that stuff off the table so we can sit down.'

Dr Paget helped Pea lift a tower of books onto the side. 'Oh hello . . . *The Famous Five*! These take me back a bit,' she said fondly.

'Yes, a bit of a theme to our bookshelves at the moment,' said Mum. 'Be warned, if you've got any devious smuggling planned, expect to be rumbled.'

Pea smiled – but Dr Skidelsky rolled her eyes and groaned.

'Not that awful Blyton woman! Surely no one still reads that rubbish?'

'That's a bit harsh,' said Mum with a giggle, patting the pile of books as if to comfort them. 'They're only books.'

'But they're *terrible* books!' said Dr Skidelsky, thumping the table so hard her oblong-framed glasses bounced on her nose. 'That dreary, boring Anne girl always stuck doing the cooking and making the beds while the boys get to be brave and adventurous. All the baddies are "swarthy", or fat, or poor – not like the snobby posh white kids we're supposed to like. The stories are all the same. And so badly written. Appalling! I can't believe you allow them in the house!'

Pea went on helping Sam One to fetch cups out of the cupboard, but she could feel her cheeks growing pinker and pinker with Dr Skidelsky's every word.

'I think other people's reading tastes are their own business, Kara dear,' said Dr Paget, gently leading Pea to a chair and plopping down next to her. 'I always rather liked them when I was little. Now, is there a knife for me to cut up this cake?'

Pea shot Dr Paget a grateful smile as she handed the plates round. Once everyone was sitting down, the conversation was smoothly steered away from books, bad or otherwise, and on to the merits of cake with raisins in, versus the sort without.

'Why have you got *Eskimo words for snow* written on your hand?' asked Tinkerbell, through a mouthful of cake.

Dr Skidelsky frowned at the scribble on the back of her hand, then slopped tea over the side of her mug. 'Argh! I meant to look that up for Chapter Three! Sorry – I'll just pop next door and—'

'Sit!' said Dr Paget.

Dr Skidelsky sat back down meekly, as if she'd been told off by the teacher. 'Sorry. It's my book. My research is all done at last, so I'm in a right old panic writing it all up.'

Dr Skidelsky was a child psychologist, and was writing a serious book based on the twins, and whether being a boy called Sam or a girl called Sam made people talk to you differently. At least, Pea thought that was what it was about.

'It's true,' whispered Sam One. 'That's why we

have to go and see our cousins, because she's gone all weird.'

Sam Two nodded. 'I found her posting the electricity bill into the toaster yesterday.'

Dr Skidelsky winced at the memory.

'Although next time that happens, Sam dear,' said Dr Paget, 'we've agreed you'll take it *out* of the toaster instead of watching it go up in flames – yes? Good. You lot must know all about having a stressed-out writer in the house. How's the latest book going, Bree? I suppose you're such an old hand these days that it just flies onto the page.'

Mum made a small squeaky noise that might have been yes, then put a big chunk of cake into her mouth.

Pea waited for her to finish it and say something else, but instead, she wedged in another even bigger piece of cake, and looked at the floor, her cheeks puffed out like a hamster.

'Um,' said Pea. 'She's writing the first *Pirate Girls* book, aren't you, Mum? It's got pirate fights, and

**37**

a flying octopus, and Coraly the ghost mermaid, and . . . er . . .'

She hesitated. She didn't know much at all about Mum's new book, apart from what had been on the rough cover picture the Dreaditor had shown them. Before, when Mum was writing the *Mermaid Girls* books, they'd sit around at breakfast and discuss what lessons mermaids had at school (scale maintenance, underwater polo, a lot of swimming), or whether short-sighted mermaids wore glasses. If it was a good writing day, Mum would skip into the kitchen when they came home from school, giddy with plot devices. If it was a bad one, they would have to tiptoe around outside the study, and occasionally deliver tea and encouraging Post-it notes.

You are definitely the best writer about mermaids there has ever been!

You are very good at typing!

If you do
250 words we will
clean the bath!

But there hadn't been any good days or bad ones lately. Pea had been so busy planning for Clover going away, and their camping trip, she hadn't really noticed – but Mum had hardly talked about the new book at all.

'She's got to give the final draft to the Dreaditor by the end of the summer holidays,' said Pea, eyeing Mum nervously.

'Well, gosh, that's . . . ages,' said Dr Paget in an encouraging voice, though she exchanged worried looks with Dr Skidelsky. 'Six whole weeks. Plenty of time. And of course you'll have them all to yourself, once you've packed these two off to the Lakes.'

Tinkerbell squashed a cherry with her fingertip. 'No she won't.'

Pea began to explain about Clem, and hospital, and pneumonia – but before she'd got very far, Mum suddenly burst into tears.

'Oh, I'm sorry, I'm so sorry – I'm crying on your lovely cherry cake!' she said, through her sobs.

'Mum?' Pea fetched her a box of tissues. 'What is it? What's wrong?'

'Oh, my pigeons, it's a disaster!' said Mum. 'There *is* no new book. I haven't written a thing!'

# THE TO-DO LIST

'That's impossible!' said Tinkerbell. 'You started writing *Pirate Girls* ages ago.'

Sam Two nodded. 'We heard loads of typing noises last time we came over.'

Mum blew her nose. 'I've been typing! Typing, and then deleting it all and typing it again, and again, because it was all rubbish. I've tried six different beginnings. I've tried starting in the middle. I've even tried writing the end first, but it just won't come out right.'

'I know that feeling,' said Dr Skidelsky sympathetically.

'Have you tried drawing pictures instead?' asked Sam One. 'That's what I do at school, if my words get stuck.'

Mum shook her head. 'These new characters – I don't know who they are, or what they'll do next. I should never have stopped writing about mermaids! And I thought it would be all right, with Clover away, and you two off with Clem, so I'd have no distractions at all . . . But now? It's hopeless!'

She looked truly distraught.

'We won't be distracting,' said Pea desperately. 'We'll be very, very quiet. And Tinkerbell will promise not to climb any ladders, or find any wasps' nests, or invent any sort of hang-glider – nothing at all that might need even a very quick trip in an ambulance – right, Tink?'

Tinkerbell looked mutinous, but eventually she nodded.

But Mum shook her head, and reached for another tissue. 'That's very sweet, Pea-nut – but of course you'll be distracting. You'll need feeding, and taking on improving trips to historical locations: that's what school holidays are for.'

'You could get a new Vitória to live here, like before, to do all that stuff,' suggested Tinkerbell.

When they had first moved to London, a Brazilian girl called Vitória had lived in their house, to take Tinkerbell to school in the mornings and look after them whenever Mum was away visiting a school, or giving one of her Creative Writing classes. After Vitória had come arty student Klaudia, then the rather gloomy Noelle – but the little private room off the kitchen had been left empty since Noelle had gone back home to France.

Mum was already shaking her head. 'We'll never find anyone in time, not now the holidays have started.'

'But you don't need to find anyone!' said Pea. It came out rather loud, and she looked down at the table, embarrassed. 'I could be the new Vitória. I know I'm not as old as Clover, but I'm not a baby. I can look after us.'

'Pea *is* a very sensible, mature young person—' Dr Paget began – but Mum stood up, knocking her chair over with a bang.

'No!' she shouted. 'You'd still be rattling around in the house. I can't just shut the door and pretend you aren't here. I need you *gone*! Properly *gone*!'

There was a terrible silence.

Tinkerbell's chin sank low into her chest, as if she might be trying to disappear.

Pea knew exactly how she felt.

With a cough, Dr Paget wondered out loud if everyone had finished their cake, and if perhaps they ought to set off for Norfolk right away.

'Enjoy your horse-riding, and your cousins,' mumbled Pea.

Sam One promised to send a postcard.

And then they were gone.

Pea sat among the empty crumby cake plates, and clutched her thumbs tightly. First Clem couldn't have them, and now Mum didn't want to.

Tinkerbell was right. This was turning out to be the worst summer holiday ever.

'We could run away to Clover's Cheese Camp,' said Tinkerbell, sucking a cherry.

They were back in the yellow tent, with Wuffly to hug, and the remains of the fruit cake. (Mum had said sorry – a lot – then had gone to lie on the red sofa, in front of a soothing-sounding TV programme about painting the walls of your house all one calm, beigy colour.)

Pea shook her head. 'We couldn't. She had to audition. You can't just turn up and ask if they mind you doing some acting at them.'

'Well, she wouldn't have to tell anyone we were there! She could hide us under her bed. She could

**45**

bring us secret picnics – stolen food all wrapped up in a bundle . . .'

It was a tempting thought. The brochure for Cheseman Hall made it look huge and Hogwarty, filled with secret passages. Pea could just imagine hiding, not under the bed but in a cobwebby attic, under constant threat of discovery – while below, Clover and all her new friends rehearsed a play. They could watch the rehearsals through a knot hole in the floorboards, to pass the time. Perhaps one of the cast would become tragically ill just before the big performance, and only someone who knew all the words could rescue the play – and Pea, having listened so patiently, so quietly, to every single rehearsal, would emerge, heroically sacrificing their hiding place to save the day . . .

Then she remembered that she hated being in plays. And that cobwebby attics had spiders, and probably inadequate toilet facilities.

'I'm not even sure where Cheseman Hall is, Tink. And how would we get there?'

'We could just start walking. Even if we didn't get all the way there, we'd find a nice empty ruined cottage, or a travelling circus, sooner or later. We could take the tent!'

Pea wondered if perhaps Tinkerbell had been reading too many Enid Blyton stories lately.

'We can't, Tink. Running away would be the most distracting thing ever.'

'But what happens if Mum doesn't ever finish her book? Will she have to give the money back? Will we have to sell our house?' Tinkerbell clung to Wuffly with a yelp. 'Will we have to sell Wuffly?'

She sounded truly frightened.

'Don't worry,' said Pea. 'It'll be fine. We'll fix it.'

But Pea, if she was perfectly honest, had no idea how.

\*

After that, the day went from bad to worse.

She tried to make comforting soup for lunch, and cut her finger chopping up an onion. (It hurt, and no one likes soup with bits of finger in.)

She tried making Mum a cup of her famous Special Writing Tea in her best spotty mug. (Mum poured it into a pot plant, then climbed back onto the sofa and pulled the duvet over her head.)

And when Pea popped out to the shops for twenty minutes, she came home to find Tinkerbell giving Wuffly a haircut on the kitchen table, with Clover's nail scissors. (Wuffly survived the experience, albeit with rather lopsided doggy eyebrows – but Pea couldn't help feeling that they were eating hairy beans on toast for dinner, which was even worse than finger soup.)

When the phone rang that evening, Pea ran to get it, fervently hoping that it would be Dr Paget to say that Norfolk was closed, and that she and the Sams were on their way back to London to rescue her.

It wasn't Dr Paget. It was Clover.

'Hello?' she said, in a whisper. 'Is that Pea? I need to talk to you very urgently.'

'I need to talk to you even more urgently!' Pea whispered back, carrying the phone into the kitchen so Mum couldn't hear. 'Help! I don't know what to do, Clover! Clem's ill so we can't go on holiday, and Mum hasn't written her book, and Tink's taken up dog-hairdressing. Everything's gone completely hopeless!'

Clover gasped down the phone. 'Oh! Should I come home? I'll come home at once.'

'No! You can't miss Cheese Camp – you've only just got there.'

'Actually, you say Cheseman Hall like *Chess*man, apparently. Everyone laughed a lot when I called it Cheese Man.'

Pea thought she could make out a little tremble in Clover's voice.

'Did they laugh in a nice way?' she asked.

There was a pause, then Clover laughed lightly down the line. 'Of course! Everyone here's *so* friendly. It's *perfectly* lovely. I'm *completely* pleased to be here. But . . . I could still come home, Pea. If you need me.'

Pea remembered the tube in Clem's hand, and Mum knocking her chair over with a bang, and her legs went wobbly.

But she'd promised Clem she would manage. Dr Paget had called her mature, and sensible. She'd wanted to be the biggest sister.

'It's no good all of us having our holidays spoiled,' she said, trying to sound brave. 'You stay there and learn Cockney urchining. We'll be all right. Only . . . what should I do? Mum's gone sort of hamsterish on the sofa. Should I phone up the Dreaditor and confess?'

'*Definitely* not. The Dreaditor mustn't find out, Pea. She'll be horrible.'

The Dreaded Editor, Nozomi Handa of Marchpane Books, usually made Mum cry, with her red-pen underlinings and crossings out, and 'Just one little suggestion, darling – just a tweak,' which always turned out to mean months of rewriting all her favourite bits. Whenever she called, Pea had to stand by with chocolate rations, and post them into Mum's mouth. And that was when Mum was at the *end* of a new book.

'What Mum needs is someone Nice, not Dreaded,' said Clover. 'A *Neditor*.'

'I could do that,' said Pea. 'I mean, I *think* I could. I could make her a sort of timetable, like at school. Oh! Or a To-Do List, so she can tick things off and feel all relieved, and get a sticker as a special reward for being a well-behaved writer.'

Recently Mum had started a sticker chart for Tinkerbell; it was pinned to the fridge, and had one column for tooth-brushing, one for bathing Wuffly, and one for *not* doing a long list of her most persistent crimes: biscuit theft, felt-pen wall art, Lego in Clover's slippers, and so on. The stickers were fruits and other shapes, with eyes and smiles, and they said things like GOOD JOB! and YOU'RE BRILLIANT! Pea had almost wanted to take up delinquency, just to earn one.

'Perfect!' said Clover. 'You'll be a brilliant Neditor, Pea.'

Pea felt warmed up, all over.

Somewhere at Clover's end, a bell rang, and she had to hurry off to the fancy Cheseman Hall dining room.

It was only after she'd gone that Pea realized she'd never found out what the very urgent thing was that Clover had called to tell her. But it would have to wait.

With a new spring in her step, Pea fetched her owl notebook from the tent, tore out a sheet, and began to write.

## MUM'S *PIRATE GIRLS* TO-DO LIST

Invent a new pirate

Make a plot plan bubble chart

Finish a chapter

Think of an especially clever metaphor

Use any of the following words:
    swashbuckle, barnacle, coracle, parrot

Write a scary bit

Keep writing until you have 1,000 words
    (proper ones, not just La-la-la-la typing)


YOU WILL GET A STICKER EACH TIME YOU DO
ONE OF THESE! GOOD LUCK!

It was a good list, she thought. A whole book seemed like a lot – but having it all written down like that made it look possible, somehow.

Pea smiled as another idea floated into her head.

She turned to the back page of her owl notebook, and wrote a new list, just for herself.

## PEA'S SUMMER HOLIDAY TO-DO LIST

Be a good Neditor for Mum
Give Tink a perfectly Famous Five holiday
Do all the things a Vitória would do
    (washing, shopping, tidying up, etc.)
Send Clem things to cheer him up

It was going to take a lot of hard work. But it would be worth it.

She awarded herself one sticker – a banana, with teeth, saying GREAT START!

It was going to be an exciting summer, after all.

# CHAPTER 5

# THE NEDITOR

**Sunday 19 July**

Dear Diary,

Today we have been being pirate girls (and a pirate dog) for inspirational purposes. Tink drew an eye-patch on her face with permanent marker.

I tried talking like a pirate all day, but it is hard to keep *Yarr*-ing and *Shiver-my-timbers*-ing when you have to ask questions like, 'Which number washing-machine cycle do sleeping bags go on if they've been trodden on by a muddy dog?' or 'If I promise to forget it again afterwards, what is your pin number so I can go to the cashpoint?' or 'How permanent is permanent marker anyway?'

Mum is still on the sofa being hamsterish in front of beige wall-painting telly,

Stickers earned by Mum: none.
Stickers earned by me: one, for cooking soup without any fingers in it.

**Monday 20 July**

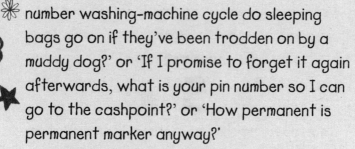

Dear Diary,
Today I wrote six pages of *The Adventures of Black-Eyed Pea*.

Mum has written NO pages.

I offered to lend her my character Rebecca Blackheart, fearsome captain of the foul ship the *Maggot*, to help her get started – but she put a cushion over her face and made squeaking noises till I went away.

I can see why the Dreaditor doesn't bother with being Nice all the time, I might try being Dreaded for a bit tomorrow.

Stickers earned by Mum: none.

Stickers earned by me: one, for taking Tinkerbell all round Tesco without her putting any Kit-Kats up her jumper; minus one because the Tesco man said her eye-patch was 'striking' so she has added a moustache and a jaggedy scar on her cheek and it turns out that permanent marker is quite permanent.

Total stickers: none.

## Tuesday 21 July

Dear Diary,

Being a Dreaditor is even harder than being a Neditor. I made Mum go and have a wash because she was starting to smell hamsterish too. Then I shouted at her a lot.

I don't think I'm very good at shouting. Mum is now in bed and she still hasn't written any words.

I tried phoning Clover to get her to teach me better voice projection, but apparently she was in the middle of a Crying lesson for if you have to do sad acting, so all I got was sniffing and hiccups.

Tinkerbell has drawn the cover of *Five Don't Ever Go on Holiday Because Life Isn't Fair*. It is a picture of Clem in his hospital bed, with some surgeons who have big saws and pointy teeth. I promised her I would post it to him, but I think a picture of flowers, kittens, etc. might be more cheering to the unwell, so I'm going to draw one of them instead.

    Stickers earned by Mum: none.
    Stickers earned by me: none.

The next morning, a postcard plopped onto the doormat. There was a picture of Norwich Castle on the front.

DEAR PEA,
NORFOLK IS COLD. WE HAVE GOT A LOT OF COUSINS. TOMORROW WE ARE GOING 'GLAMPING', WHICH MEANS 'GLAMOROUS CAMPING' WHERE YOU HAVE A BED IN YOUR TENT AND ELECTRIC LIGHTS AND WI-FI. I HAVE NOT HAD TO GO ON A HORSE YET.

FROM SAM

Tinkerbell sighed at it enviously all through breakfast.

Later, Pea found her in the garden with Wuffly, trying to make the cord of the table lamp stretch all the way out to the tent. (It didn't.)

'Proper Famous Five-ish camping doesn't need electricity,' Pea said. 'It's cheating, like pillows.'

Tinkerbell was not convinced, so Pea took her to the library to get out some more real *Famous Five* books and check them for Wi-Fi.

As she looked through the shelves, trying to remember which ones they'd already borrowed, Dr Skidelsky's words rumbled guiltily around in her stomach.

*Terrible books!*

*All the same.*

*So badly written.*

*Can't believe you allow them in the house!*

Dr Skidelsky was the brainiest person Pea knew. If she said Enid Blyton books were bad for you, did that mean they were? Anne *did* always stay behind to fuss about making the caravan look neat and tidy. The other girl in the Famous Five, George, was brilliant and brave and just as good as a boy (the books said that lots of times) . . . did that mean the books were trying to say being a girl wasn't ever good? And it was true, after all, that all the good characters were from 'nice' families, with a mother and father, and pots of money. Enid would never have written a book about a family like Pea's, or the Paget-Skidelskys.

Even lovely Miss Pond, the school librarian, had given her a very severe look when she'd asked for a *Malory Towers* or two to take home for Tinkerbell a few weeks ago, and directed her to a shelf full of thick tomes: 'proper' books for a 'confident reader' like Pea.

It was the same with Mum's *Mermaid Girls*. Some people were awfully suspicious about mermaids.

And girls. Once, she'd been behind a girl in a bookshop queue who was clutching *Mermaid Girls 2: Deeper Water*, and had hopped excitedly from one foot to the other, trying to muster the courage to introduce herself – only to see the girl's dad pluck the book out of her hands in horror, and exchange it for something less sparkly.

There was a big poster in Miss Pond's library which said LOVE READING! Pea did. But were there special rules about which bits of reading she was allowed to love?

It was all very confusing.

Not that Tinkerbell was bothered. She sat on the library floor, carefully scanning the descriptions on the back covers. She chose *Five Have Plenty of Fun* – 'It says George gets kidnapped in this one!' – and *Five Get into Trouble* – 'And Dick gets kidnapped in this one!' – and had already finished a whole chapter by the time Pea had picked out her own selection (*Pirateology*, and *Pirate Girl*, and

**62**

*Pirates!* for Neditorial inspiration – and *Ballet Shoes* to re-read, for comfortingness).

If Enid Blyton made Tinkerbell happy, Pea decided, she was helpful for the To-Do List, so it was probably all right – and anyway, Dr Skidelsky didn't have to know.

Back at home, Pea made Mum another mug of Special Writing Tea, turned off the beige-walls programme, and wedged a pencil into Mum's floppy hand.

'I want at least three sentences, or no sticker for you again today!' she said sternly.

Then she took Mum's mobile phone out to the tent, and called Clover.

'Help!' she whispered. 'It's not working! I don't think mums care as much about stickers as children do. And I've tried being Dreaded, but she just lies on the sofa, all flop.'

'Oh no,' said Clover in a muffled voice. 'Should I come home, do you think?'

'No, you mustn't – Mum would hate you to miss learning urchining and all the rest.' She hesitated as Clover made a snotty sort of noise. 'Are you all right? Have you been to Crying lessons again?'

'Yes, that's right,' said Clover eventually, noisily blowing her nose. 'I'm getting ever so good at it – everyone says so.'

Pea sighed. 'Is it really like Hogwarts there?'

'Sort of. I mean, we aren't learning magic spells and no one's been murdered.'

'Is there posh food?'

'Hmm? Oh. Yes, of course! It's all ever so grand. Roast chicken and gravy every night.' Pea's stomach rumbled enviously.

Ever since she'd taken over the cooking, there had been a lot of toast on the menu – and while everyone liked toast, she was running out of things to put on top of it.

'Inspiration, that's what Mum needs,' said

Clover, before she had to hurry off to her next class. 'Like a magical light bulb, popping on over her head.'

But poor Pea had no idea where to find one.

Even working on her own story didn't help: *The Adventures of Black-Eyed Pea* was stuck in a long boring scene where Pirate Pea lay in her hammock feeling seasick.

After an hour of staring at the next blank page, she wandered back inside.

The clicky sound of typing drifted out from the study, and her heart leaped with hope – but it was only Tinkerbell.

'Look at this!' she said, spinning in Mum's office chair. 'Enid Blyton wrote *hundreds* of books. Sometimes she wrote a whole one every week! Mum's just being a big lazy rubbish.'

On the screen was a website showing book covers, and a black-and-white photo of Enid herself. She didn't look at all like Mum. She was older, with dark curled hair, pearls around her neck and a neat little collar. Although she was smiling softly, she looked quite serious and stern.

'That was a long time ago,' said Pea, feeling defensive. 'Maybe there were more spare book ideas floating around back then. If Enid hadn't used up so many, Mum would probably be fine.'

It didn't sound very sensible, even as she said it. Tinkerbell gave her a withering look, and marched out to read more kidnapping.

Pea slipped into the spinny chair, and clicked her way around the website, smiling each time she saw a book she recognized.

The numbers were true. Enid Blyton had written so many books, no one could even count them, since the same stories popped up in different places. What was obvious was how much people loved her, though. Mum had a website where people could write messages, and she got boxes of 'Marina Mail', sent on from the Dreaditor. But here on Enid Blyton's website were comments and messages from people all over the world who loved the books.

Tinkerbell had typed up a new comment too.

```
I like when they go to a secret cave with a sandy
bottom and sleep in it by themselves without
grown-ups and have campfires and like a whole
loaf of bread and a meat pie George is the best
one Anne is stupid but I still like them from
Tinkerbell Llewellyn age 8 and 1/6
```

Pea started to type her own message in the comments box, but then she remembered Dr Skidelsky again, and felt self-conscious – and then guilty for worrying if someone saw her name.

She went to fetch her owl notebook instead.

Dear Enid Blyton,

I read on your website that you're dead, so this isn't a letter that you'll ever get, but I still wanted to write to you to say sorry for what Dr Skidelsky said about you being terrible. You are not! (Although some of your books are not very practical, e.g. caves are not often sandy-bottomed, they are mostly sort of cold and drippy on the inside. And it is a shame that Anne always has to do the washing-up.)

I wish you weren't dead so I could ask you how you wrote so many books. I think there must have been some sort of magical Blyton fumes in the air where you lived so you breathed in book ideas all the time, because Mum is taking for ever to just think of one. If there are Blyton fumes, please send us some.

Love from Pea xx

Then she tucked her feet up under herself on the spinny chair, and clicked through more of the website.

She read all about Enid, and her real life. She'd had daughters, like Mum, though only two, and a dog called Bobs. She'd borrowed bits of her own life, just like Mum did: her second husband was called Kenneth Fraser Darrell Waters, like Darrell Rivers in the *Malory Towers* books. She had a house called Green Hedges, just like the twins at *St Clare's*.

Pea clicked on a photo: an old ruined castle on a green hill. *Corfe Castle, said to be the model for Kirrin Castle*, said the caption below.

Kirrin Castle in the books was on an island, and belonged to George. The real castle wasn't on an island, but you could visit it and wander around. There were pictures of it at night too, all lit up as if waiting for a ghost to haunt the tumbled-down walls. At the bottom of the page was another caption:

*Enid and her family regularly holidayed in Swanage, and visited Corfe Castle village many times. The village now contains a specialist shop, selling Blyton books and memorabilia, and Blyton fans travel from all over the world to see the landscape which inspired these wonderful stories.*

Pea felt an excited little skip in her heart.

*Inspiration* – that's what Clover said Mum needed. If anywhere had Blyton fumes in the air, it had to be Corfe Castle. And Tinkerbell would love to go on a Famous Five-ish trip, to the very place where George and Timmy the dog had run about solving mysteries and foiling kidnappers.

She clicked away from the Enid Blyton page and onto a map, to see if it was impossibly far away – but Corfe Castle was down in Dorset on the south coast of England, much nearer than the Lake District; just a few hours away by train.

Twenty minutes later, she summoned Tinkerbell

and Wuffly to the front room, switched off the TV, and ordered Mum to sit up and listen.

'Now, I'm your Neditor, so you have to do what I say. We should go on holiday.'

Mum stared, bewildered, as Pea pressed a printed sheet from the internet into her hands. On it was a small photo of a grey stone cottage.

'Pea-pod, I have a book to write, I can't possibly—'

'A *working* holiday,' Pea said quickly. 'In the most inspiring place in the whole world! It's only seven miles from the sea too, so that'll help with the pirate bits. And there's a castle, and lots for us to do, so we wouldn't be distracting. That cottage backs onto a common, and there are bunk beds, and a wood-burning stove – a bit like an indoor campfire.'

Tinkerbell's eyes lit up.

'There's room in the back garden for a tent, if we want to do some almost-camping. And they let you bring a dog, so Wuffly can come. The website says they've just had a cancellation, and it's available to rent for the next two weeks, starting Friday! I thought we could use the Granny Duff money to pay for it all. It worked for Enid Blyton, Mum.'

Tinkerbell clung onto Mum's elbows and ran on the spot. 'Can we, Mum? Can we *please*?'

Mum frowned at the printed page, but she was already pushing her hamsterish duvet nest aside, a smile creeping across her face.

'Yes, my swans,' she said, her eyes beginning to sparkle. 'Yes. We're going on holiday after all!'

# CHAPTER 6

# OFF TO CORFE CASTLE

It was quite a thrill to wake up, three days later, in the bottom bunk of a whole new bedroom.

(There had been some discussion as to who would get the top bunk. Pea felt it was very noble and big sisterly of her to allow Tinkerbell the privilege, and had awarded herself two stickers and a biscuit.)

When they ran downstairs, on the doormat by their new, temporary front door they found two letters waiting for them.

The first was a card from Clem.

Inside were two crisp ten-pound notes.

'I'm going to spend mine all on fudge,' said Tinkerbell, sniffing the money.

Pea hesitated. She quite wanted to see what ten pounds' worth of fudge looked – and tasted – like herself, but she was sure Vitória wouldn't have allowed it.

'I'll look after that,' said Pea, tucking both notes into her little spotted purse and hoping she sounded grown up. 'We're here for two weeks, remember. You might see something else you really want.'

'What could I possibly want more than fudge?'

Pea ignored her, and picked up the other letter. It had blue forget-me-nots all around the edge of the envelope, and Clover's familiar curly handwriting.

Dear beautiful family!

Hello! How is your cottage? Mum wasn't sure if you would have the internet, so I am sending you a real letter to welcome you to your new holiday home. (Did you know that first-class stamps cost 62p each? For one letter! 62p is two Coconut Rings from the Cheseman Hall afternoon tuck shop, just so you know the sacrifice I am making. But I will write you a lovely long one to make it feel like a sound financial investment.)

In case you were even a tiny bit slightly worried about me, I've made ever so many friends already. My very best friend is Agata, who has fluffy blonde hair — everyone says we look like twins.

My room is called Pawns 3 (everything is named after chess pieces here) because I'm new this year. I'm sharing with seven darling little girls. I have one of the bottom bunks. Agata is in Queens, which is the building with lots of fancy single rooms where all the other girls my age are. Agata says if I come back another year then I might be in Queens too. She's been coming to Cheseman since she was ten and has been on Holby City as a wan-faced immigrant. (That proves what a good actor she is as she is not wan-faced at all.)

In Characterization we are exploring facial microexpressions to broaden our emotional palette for close-up television work. Candace (she's the teacher) gives you a card with your emotion on it and then holds a cardboard frame over your face so some of it is covered up. I had to display Apathy using only my chin. Candace said I made 'a heroic effort'.

Sorry, I had to go to dinner just then.

Tink, I'm ever so sorry but I'm not in Sword-fighting class. When Sword-fighting class is on we small Pawns are all doing Introduction to Period Dancing (which isn't what it sounds like), or Dialects (that means accents, though we haven't done Cockney urchin yet). Our Small Group Work is to write and perform a short dramatic piece based on a famous painting. Agata's group have a painting of a tiger in some spiky leaves. The Bishop group has ballerinas. My group has a bowl of fruit on a table. I am to be Third Banana.

I MISS YOU ALL! But of course I'm having utterly the most wonderful time and you mustn't worry about me one bit or phone me up to check I'm all right because obviously I completely am. Please write back AT ONCE to tell me all your adventures.

Kisses,
Clover x

Once they were washed, dressed and breakfasted, they sat in their bunk beds to write replies.

Dear Dad,
Thank you for the money. I am actually going to spend it on fudge.

Tink xxxxxxxxxxxxxx
P.S. Get well soon

Pea wrote back to Clover.

Dear Clover,

Yes, we are here in Corfe Castle village! I think you would really love it here (though probably not as much as Period Dancing, Chin Apathy, etc.). Our house is called Rosebud Cottage and it has:

&#10047; a living room with big flowery sofas and a wooden table for Mum to write at

&#10047; a kitchen which had a loaf of bread and a bottle of wine in it for us when we arrived (I thought they might have been left behind by mistake but Mum said it was a present from the owner; I hope she's right because we have eaten the bread)

✿ a garden with a patio, and a shed
with an old wooden sledge in it, and a gate
at the end which opens onto a gigantic
common that goes all the way to the castle!
(Also there is room for us to put the tent up
but we haven't yet because it got quite
wet when we took it down at home and
there wasn't time for it to dry before we
packed so it is hanging in the bathroom
like a big yellow bat – Tinkerbell said
that bit)

✿ bunk beds for me and Tinkerbell, like
you have at Cheseman Hall

✿ a giant double bed for Mum

✿ a bathroom (with a wet tent in it)

✿ a corner of hallway for Wuffly's bed

❀ a cupboard full of jigsaws, rubbish DVDs, and a board game called *Remonstrate!* with lots of plastic bits and no instructions

❀ about a thousand million Enid Blyton books (Tinkerbell said that bit too)

And those are just inside the house. We arrived quite late so have only been on a walk to the pub for dinner last night so far (I had chicken Kiev with chips and salad), but we saw the castle. It is about five minutes away from our garden gate. It is very ruined-looking, but I expect it has dungeons, etc. We're going to visit it today!

Tink says:

Best Thing – bunk beds

Worst Thing – the train didn't sell ginger beer so we haven't had any lashings of that yet

We have to go out now so Mum can be inspired by all the Blyton fumes. I am in charge of the mobile phone and making sure Tink doesn't die.

We miss you! Good luck with being Third Banana.


Love from Pea xx


Then they signed each other's letters.

Pea went to ask for stamps – but Mum was sitting at the scrubbed wooden table, the old laptop she'd borrowed from Dr Skidelsky humming before her. Her *Pirate Girls* To-Do List was beside her, and there was a Post-it note stuck to her hair.

*DO NOT DISTURB*

*Blyton fumes at work!*

Pea left her a message on the back of Clover's envelope.

I am not disturbing. I am just telling you we are going out now. We will bring back lunch things.

Yes, I have the mobile phone.

Happy writing!

Love from your Neditor XX

Pea patted her pockets carefully (mobile phone, spotty purse, house key), then steered Tinkerbell to the door.

'Wuffly on the lead, remember, Tink.'

'It's Timmy now, not Wuffly – like the Famous Five's dog in the books. Come on, Timmy, here's your lead. Timmy? Tim? Timothy?'

Wuffly circled their legs, oblivious.

'I don't think Wuffly knows she's called Timmy now, Tink.'

'She'll learn,' said Tinkerbell cheerfully. 'Come along, Tim, let's go and find a mystery to solve!'

The sky was grey with cloud and the pavements were wet, but it had stopped raining for the moment. Pea breathed in the smell of damp grass and earth. Was that what Blyton fumes smelled like? It was only a road – an ordinary road lined with terraced stone houses – but there was a thrill in the air, somehow. It was a road with a castle at the end of it. The possibilities were endless.

The village was small, with three roads leading to a war memorial in a tiny square filled with summer Saturday tourists, and a little station with steam trains to Swanage. Pea slipped into the post office to get stamps, and Tinkerbell dropped their letters into the post box. Just next door was the special Enid Blyton shop, stuffed full of books and memorabilia – but Tinkerbell marched past, tugging Wuffly-Tim's lead. She even ignored the huge sweet shop.

'Fudge later,' she said. 'Castle first.'

But when they turned up the driveway, there was a large sign and a gate barring their way. Off to the side was a building painted white, with flags hanging from the high ceiling like an old banqueting hall. There were people in costume inside – a knight in silver armour, a peasant woman in a long blue dress – and a queue of people, all lining up to buy tickets.

'You have to *pay* to go in?'

To Pea's horror, Tinkerbell's disgusted voice was loud enough to catch the attention of one of the dressed-up people. Her short brown hair was tucked under her hat, and she wore a flowing white shirt and high leather boots. In her hand was a longbow, and there was a quiver of real arrows slung over her green woollen cape.

'I'm afraid so, gentle traveller,' she said with a chuckle.

Then she posed, with her bow drawn; as a passing tourist took her photograph. 'Eliza Hood, castle archer, at your service!' she said, slapping her thigh.

'Um. Pleased to meet you,' said Pea nervously.

'Why do we have to pay?' Tinkerbell whispered. 'How are we going to have Famous Five adventures and solve mysteries in the dungeons if we have to pay?'

Pea didn't know. She'd imagined them running around the deserted castle ruins all by themselves, just like in the books – but there were hundreds of people coming in and out, and a whole medieval village set up inside the gates.

'If you're planning to visit more than once, perhaps, gentles, you might be interested in membership?' said Eliza the archer, and reached under her cape to hand Pea a printed leaflet with a form on the back. 'Needs an adult to sign it, though,' she added with a wink.

Pea took it, feeling more hopeful – if a little

confused about being given a form to fill in by someone from history. The leaflet said that membership was for a whole year, to lots of different castles and fancy houses. But it was much, much more than Clem's pocket money could cover.

'Have we got enough just to go in for today?' whispered Tinkerbell, her eyes very large and pleading.

Pea shook her head. 'We do. But we might only visit it once, now we know you need tickets – and it would be mean to go without Mum.'

'You could phone her, and tell her to come and meet us?'

Pea shook her head again. 'Do not disturb the Blyton fumes – remember?'

They walked up the path as far as the fenced-off entrance.

There was a sudden chill in the air. The wind began to rise. Beyond the gatehouse, the castle loomed against fast-moving dark clouds, tumble-down walls and towers gazing imperiously down from the hill. Inside the fence, children ran across the grass dressed up as knights in chain mail, wielding wooden swords and yelling with delight.

There was a low rumble of thunder, and it began to rain: fat heavy raindrops that splashed straight through Pea's trainers. She and Tinkerbell zipped up their raincoats and pulled up their hoods, watching as the tiny Crusaders ran to shelter in a large white tent.

Pea gazed up at the blank windows in the highest tower of the castle as lightning flashed across the sky. If this was an Enid Blyton story, this would be the moment when a mysterious face appeared at a window: a kidnapped scientist, or a sneaky smuggler trying to hide.

But there was no mysterious face. Even if there had been, they couldn't get inside the castle to see it.

'It's not fair,' murmured Tinkerbell.

*No*, thought Pea, *it really isn't*. This wasn't like being in a book at all.

# CHAPTER 7

# RECRUITING

There was a crackle, and lightning flashed across the clouds again.

Wuffly howled, straining on her lead, while Tinkerbell frantically tried to calm her.

There was another long shuddery rumble of thunder that seemed to roll around over their heads – followed almost at once by another flash.

'Pea! Come on! We have to get Wuff— I mean, *Timmy* inside.'

They couldn't get back to the cottage now, not with Wuffly whining and quivering. Pea liked thunderstorms – the way the air seemed to vibrate around you – but they reduced Wuffly to a frightened tangle of legs and stiff fur. She usually vanished under a bed or into a cupboard. Once, in their old flat in Tenby, they'd been unable to find her again once the sky had cleared – until Mum went to finish putting on a load of laundry, and found her burrowed into a bundle of bed linen inside the washing machine. After that, it had become family policy to always check the drum for dog before shutting the door.

They ran back towards the square, and ducked into the first doorway they came to: the Castle Tea Rooms.

It was already full of other soaking wet tourists – but it was indoors, and warm, and there were tables for Wuffly to hide under.

Pea hurried Tinkerbell to a corner table and studied the menu.

'Look! Ginger beer, just like the real Famous Five. We can still be Blyton-ish, even if we're not in the castle.'

She went up to the counter and ordered two ginger beers, and a toasted teacake for them to share. It felt very grown up, being the one in charge of such decisions.

The ginger beer arrived in brown glass bottles with a straw poked into the neck, and Tinkerbell perked up at once – but the moment she tried it her face crinkled up in disgust.

'Yuck! This tastes like dust on fire. No way did the Famous Five drink lashings of that!'

Pea had to admit she didn't much like it either, but she kept taking small sips in the hope that it would get less horrible.

'We could go on the steam train later?' said Pea. 'That's Blyton-ish.'

Tinkerbell stuck out her bottom lip. 'I went on a train *yesterday*.'

The mobile phone hummed in Pea's pocket.

It was Mum, who had apparently only just noticed the lightning and thunder and realized that her children were out in it. Pea took this as a good sign, Neditorially speaking, and promised they were tucked up safe and having a wonderful adventure.

'No we're not,' said Tinkerbell, after Pea had hung up. She stroked Wuffly's still-whimpery nose with a damp sleeve. 'This place is *rubbish*. No one's going to kidnap us or lock us in a dungeon here.'

'Good! You're not supposed to *want* to be kidnapped or locked in a dungeon, Tink.'

'But those are the best bits! Then I could be totally brave and good at escaping.'

Pea frowned. She'd promised Clem to give Tinkerbell a perfectly Blyton-ish holiday. She could manage a tent and ginger beer – even if it was horrible. But arranging a kidnapping?

'Anyway, how can we be Famous Fivey when there's only three of us?' Tinkerbell asked.

'We'll just have to make some new friends.'

Tinkerbell sat up. 'There were adverts pinned up in the post-office window. We could advertise for the other two – and have interviews to see who's good enough.'

Pea thought that this was a fairly extreme approach to making new friends, but Tinkerbell looked brighter, so she just nodded.

Eventually the thundery rumbles blew over, and the rain stopped.

They went back to the castle gates. There was a muddy path running around the mound, outside the fence.

Pea kept her eyes peeled for sinister footprints or fallen scraps of paper with clues on, but there was no sign of an exciting mystery to solve; only a disappointingly sensible, friendly 'Nature Trail' curving back off the road at the bottom of the mound, full of information about squirrels.

Meanwhile Tinkerbell scanned passers-by for adventurous potential.

'What about them?' she said, pointing at a family walking ahead of them: a mum and two girls who trailed behind her. 'Though it ought to be boys, really, to make it properly Famous Fivey.'

As the girls got closer, one pulled the other one's hair, and was pinched in return, and then they had a shouty fight using quite rude words.

Pea shook her head, and hurried on past.

The next family they came to had a baby and a toddler.

'Too small,' declared Tinkerbell.

They met the perfect family – two Japanese children about Pea's age with their grandparents, all in new-looking matching waterproofs and practical hiking boots – but they spoke no English at all, and after Tinkerbell's attempt to mime the word *kid-napping*, they waved nervously and hurried away.

They followed the path back up the slope as it looped round to meet the castle mound again, but there wasn't another soul on the trail.

'What we really need is a den,' said Tinkerbell thoughtfully. 'Probably, if there's a really good one, the best sort of people to join our Famous Five will already have found it for us and be waiting in it with heather and rugs and a campfire. We should look for smoke!'

Tinkerbell charged into the wet undergrowth after Wuffly.

The village lay in a valley, with two steep hills rising up from either side of the castle mound. One hill had a clear path all the way to the top, with steps cut into the hillside at the steepest point. There was no sign of campfire smoke, but it seemed a likely spot.

They struggled up the hill, skidding on the muddiest parts. Tinkerbell veered off the path to explore each encouraging-looking clump of brambles, but with no success. Once they got to the flattish top, they stopped to catch their breath, shivering in the wind.

There was no handy ruined cottage, no hidden entrance to a cave. Pea looked hopefully at a large hollow dip in the ground, with a weather-beaten tree curled protectively over it – but there was nothing but a smelly cowpat at the bottom.

'At least the view's nice?' she said, looking at the castle, and far in the distance, the sea, dotted with little boats.

Tinkerbell – who had begun to go slightly bluish around the mouth – gave her a look, her teeth chattering.

Pea couldn't blame her. If this was one of the books, there would be chocolate in her pocket, or perhaps a packet of biscuits. But she hadn't thought of it. Perhaps she didn't deserve to be in their Famous Five, either; not even as boring sensible Anne.

They slipped and skidded back down the hill, and into the woods again. There was a wooden sign pointing out different paths, but they headed back the way they'd come, over a bridge.

'What's hairy, bites people, and grows antlers at the full moon? Over.'

The voice floated up from underneath the bridge: a boy's, with what Pea was fairly sure was a Scottish accent.

She and Tinkerbell both peeped over the side of the bridge, but could see no one; just a lower wooden footbridge, crossing the stream a little further down. There was a boy with a messy swoop of dark hair up ahead, though, standing some distance away along the curve of the road. He wore black sunglasses and some sort of uniform: combat trousers, a utility belt covered with pouches, and a black hoodie with a round green logo on the front. He was holding something square and silver with his left hand, waving it about over his head. Then he tucked the silver thing into his belt and, with the same hand, reached across himself to another pocket, and took out a walkie-talkie.

His voice echoed up from under the bridge, filtered through static; the same accent, but older and slightly weary. 'I don't know, Agent Troy. What's hairy, bites people, and grows antlers at the full moon? Over.'

'A deerwolf! What's hairy, bites people, and waves pompoms at the full moon? Over.'

There was another crackle of static. 'I don't know, Agent Troy—'

'A cheerwolf! What's hairy, bites people, and goes to the pub at the full moon? Over.'

There was silence.

Tinkerbell wrinkled her nose, then leaned further over the edge of the bridge.

'A beerwolf?' she suggested.

There was a yelp, and a splashy sound echoed from under the bridge.

'Don't tell me you've dropped your walkie-talkie in the water again, Agent Troy.'

There was more splashing. 'No! Well, yes. But it works . . . if you can hear this. Can you hear this? Over.'

'Yes, I can hear you, you numpty. Any readings?'

'I don't know. There's two Unknown Human Entities and a dog up on the bridge, so I'm very secretly waiting underneath till they go away.'

Pea squeaked and clapped her hand over her

mouth. Wuffly let out a loud bark, as if she knew she was being discussed.

'Sorry!' said Tinkerbell, hanging her head over the side of the bridge. 'We didn't mean to be Unknown Human Entities!'

There was an awkward silence.

'Do I take it that was one of the UHES, Agent Troy? Over.'

'Um. Yes. Over.'

There was an audible sigh through the walkie-talkie. 'Abort covert mission, report to Agent Dad for debrief. I swear, little brother, at this rate we are *never* going to track down this ghost.'

# CHAPTER 8

# PIE

'Ghost?' Pea felt a tingle run down her spine. 'Did he say they're tracking a ghost?'

Tinkerbell leaned even further over the edge of the bridge, eagerly peering down into the stream. 'Hello?'

A head appeared from under the bridge: a boy about Tinkerbell's age, with shorter brown hair, also wearing sunglasses – though he appeared to be wearing his over the top of a pair of ordinary spectacles. He produced a silver box like the one the other boy held, and pointed it at Tinkerbell's head. It buzzed, then made a sort of squealing noise.

'Aha!' he said excitedly. 'Agent Ryan! The UHEs have a very high EMF reading . . . That's electro-magnetic field,' he added, splashing out of the stream and scrambling up the bank. 'Agent Ryan! Shall I wake up Agent Dad?'

Pea suddenly realized that there was a huge man sitting in a folding chair, over on the other bank. He wore a funny blue fisherman's cap that was slightly too small for his head, had a thick fuzz of gingery beard all around the bottom of his chin, quite a round tummy – and he was fast asleep.

'No need,' said the older boy with the swoopy hair, Ryan, joining them on the bridge. Pea guessed he was eleven or twelve, and she got the feeling he was rather embarrassed that their dad was there, snoozing away, when Pea and Tinkerbell were out by themselves.

Tinkerbell made the introductions, while Wuffly gave both boys an interrogatory sniff.

'Pea, Tinkerbell . . .' said Ryan, looking them up and down. 'Codenames, eh? Interesting.'

'Um,' said Pea. 'No. Those are our actual names.'

It wasn't strictly true. Tinkerbell was Tinkerbell thanks to Mum leaving a small Clover and Pea in charge of naming their new baby sister. (They were in a fairy phase at the time.) But Pea's real name was Prudence, an unfortunate choice for a girl who developed a lisp. When introducing herself as 'Pwudenthe' became tiresome, a kindly teacher had called her 'Pea' for short. The lisp had gone, but the Pea had stuck.

'If you say so,' said Ryan, clearly not believing her. 'We'd take the same precautions ourselves, if we weren't here on official business – right, Agent Troy?'

Troy had knelt down and was cheerfully letting Wuffly lick his glasses – both pairs – but now he leaped up, and together the boys performed an intricate sort of handshake: left hands clasped, elbows tapped together twice, then left fists bumped into the other's shoulder, finishing with the wrists raised up and a shout of 'Pie!' They both wore a neon-green plastic loop, like a flat jelly bracelet, around one wrist, with the letters PIE written on it in black marker. The neon-green circle on their hoodies bore the same initials, inside a simple, slightly wonky drawing of a ghost.

'Pie?' said Pea.

'Paranormal Investigations Edinburgh,' Ryan said, then added, in a quieter voice, 'Troy chose the name.'

'*And* designed the wee ghostie logo,' Troy said, proudly tapping the symbol on his hoodie.

'So you're, like, ghost hunters?' asked Tinkerbell.

'Ghosts, for sure. Any and all forms of supernatural activity. Haunted houses, poltergeists, vampires . . .'

'You believe in *vampires*?'

'You don't?'

Pea and Tinkerbell both giggled – but the boys seemed perfectly serious.

'Ghosts are just made up and stupid,' said Tinkerbell, trying to tug Wuffly away from fondly chewing Troy's trainer laces. 'If spooky stuff was really real, we'd see it all the time, not just at Halloween – and it wouldn't be all the obvious things, either. There'd be vampire kittens and werewolf dolphins—'

'Who says there aren't?' said Ryan.

'I do! No one ever sees a ghost spider, or a ghost bird, or a ghost fish.'

'Aha!' Troy beamed. 'We have. Just last year we spent a whole week tracking down the Phantom Squid of Musselburgh. There's a video of it on our website and everything.'

Ryan cleared his throat. 'Though strictly speaking, that was a ghost mollusc, not a fish,' he said, peering over the top of his sunglasses.

Pea caught his eye and smiled. It was the sort of thing she might have said herself, if someone got the details wrong about a *Mermaid Girls* book. She liked it when other people wanted facts to be right too – even if they were the made-up sort of facts.

'So you've not had a PPS, then? A Potential Paranormal Sighting?' said Troy, waving the silver box near each of them in turn, as if scanning them. It buzzed especially loudly when it got near Pea's hair, and she recoiled. 'Are you quite sure?'

'Duh,' said Tinkerbell. 'I think we'd have noticed.'

But the two boys weren't listening; they were too busy muttering about whatever the silver box had picked up.

'What do you think, Agent Troy? The Grey Lady?'

There was a Grey Lady ghost in the *Harry Potter* books, but according to the boys, this one was quite different. She was supposed to haunt the village square – and, so the local legend went, she had no head.

Pea patted her possibly-haunted hair, alarmed.

'She's why Dad picked Corfe Castle to come on holiday,' said Ryan, pushing his sunglasses back up.

Troy nodded. 'There's meant to be a White Woman as well – that's a lady in her nightie – but almost everywhere has one of those. The Grey Lady's the one we came to see.'

Tinkerbell snorted. 'Well, we don't believe in phantom squids, or grey ladies,' she scoffed. '*We* picked to come here on holiday to solve a real mystery, not a made-up one. Well, and to help our mum write her book – but mainly the mystery thing. Like the Famous Five.'

To their astonishment, the boys had never heard of Enid Blyton, or the Famous Five.

'Are you sure they're famous? What do they *do*?' asked Troy.

'Eating, mainly,' said Pea.

'And catching villains. We're just like them, only there aren't five of us. We've got a tent, and lashings of ginger beer – though it turns out that's horrible. You could forget all your silly PIE ghostie business and join us instead,' Tinkerbell added casually. 'Just to make up the numbers. If you wanted.'

Pea found herself very much wishing these two odd boys with their peculiar gadgets would say yes.

But Ryan shook his head. 'Uh, no thanks. We're professionals. We don't have time to waste on non-believers. Right, Agent Troy?'

'*Dead* right,' said Troy.

They did their funny handshake again, then set off across the bridge, Troy hurrying ahead to tell their dad all about the UHEs and their dog.

'Paranormal investigators – pff,' said Tinkerbell. 'They're going to be so sorry they didn't join us when we find a *real* mystery to solve.'


'Oh, Mum. What *have* you been doing?' said Pea, staring at the scrubbed wooden table in the cottage's living room.

Pea had stopped in the village to buy pasties from the bakery, and then they'd hurried home for lunch, hoping to find Mum surrounded by new piratical notes and ideas. The borrowed laptop was humming away – but it was pushed to one side, to make space for an enormous half-finished jigsaw.

Mum hung her head. 'I wrote a whole paragraph. Then I found that in the cupboard and got a teeny bit distracted. Hang on – what have *you* been doing?'

Pea looked at their reflections in the mirror. Their trainers and jeans were crusted over with mud from their walk, and Pea's hair had blown into a sort of ginger halo of frizz, with leaves in. Wuffly was even filthier.

'We've been looking for a mystery,' said Tinkerbell, finding a towel before Wuffly could tread mucky prints all over the flowery sofa. 'But we couldn't find one. We couldn't go in the castle. And we met some stupid Scottish boys.'

'They weren't *stupid*,' said Pea.

'They've never even heard of Enid Blyton! And they believe in ghosts. Troy's jokes are rubbish. And Ryan's got a funny hand.'

'Tink!' Pea glared at her, hard. 'Don't. That's mean.'

'But he does! He's got a funny hand, and his arm's all stiff, and he walks funny too. I'm not being mean, Mum – he *does*.'

Mum raised an eyebrow and looked at Pea.

Pea felt her face go hot. She hadn't really noticed at first; she was too busy wondering what the green logo meant and envying Ryan's sunglasses. (Pea's sunglasses had come free in a magazine and had green plastic frames shaped like palm-tree leaves. Clover had declared them 'magnificent', and Pea thought of the word every time she put them on – but Ryan's were plain black all over, like Mum's, and she had a feeling that might mean his were better.) But when the boys had done their complicated handshake-thing, she realized that Ryan's right hand had a sort of rubbery fingerless glove that went up under his sleeve, and his small fingers were all curled up. When he held the walkie-talkie and the silver box, he'd reached across himself with his left hand, even though it was awkward; his right arm just hung there, except when he sort of hugged it close. He walked differently too, with a bit of a limp.

Once she'd noticed it, Pea had watched with her heart in her mouth, hoping Tinkerbell wouldn't say anything loud and accidentally rude, and worrying that she herself might get caught staring. Was she supposed to have said something? Was it rude *not* to have said something? Was it rude to be talking about him now?

'Well, unless it told you a joke, I doubt he has a *funny* hand,' said Mum, smiling gently at them both. 'Maybe you should ask him what he calls it – that might be nicer for him. And if he doesn't want to talk about it, then that's fine too. Really, all that matters is if he's nice. Is he nice?'

Pea nodded. 'A bit weird. Oh! Not because of . . . I mean – I think they're nice-weird. Like us.'

Tinkerbell scrunched up her face. 'They were total stupid-heads! We're not being friends with them. Anyway, I've decided five is too many people to fit in our tent, so we don't need to be the Famous Five. We're going to be the, um . . .'

'Terrible Two?' suggested Mum.

'Mum! Wuffly-Tim totally counts.'

'Of course she does, Stinks. Um . . . the Thoughtful Three?'

'The *Thrilling* Three?' said Pea.

'Yes!' said Tinkerbell. 'That's us. Now, where is lunch? Even though the Thrilling Three aren't the Famous Five, we can probably eat exactly as much as they would.'

They ate pasties sitting by the wood-burner, with Mum's turquoise-painted toenails wiggling on the hearth as she typed. They spent the afternoon finishing off Mum's jigsaw while she worked, so she couldn't be tempted.

That night, Pea left mum writing and read the start of *Five on a Hike Together* for Tinkerbell's bedtime story herself. Then she sat in her bunk, composing a letter.

Dear Enid Blyton,

Please explain why none of your books
have people getting freezing cold after a
thunderstorm, or having to pay to go into
castles.

Also I think you have overestimated how
much children like ginger beer.

I still love you, though.

Your fumes are working! Mum has written
two whole chapters already. I gave her a
sticker with a watermelon that says, SUPER!
and she stuck it on the edge of the laptop,
even though it is a borrowed one from Dr
Skidelsky. I'm not sure Dr Skidelsky will like
having a laptop with a watermelon on it but I
don't like to be discouraging.

If Blyton fumes could also bring me a
kidnapped scientist or some buried treasure
for the Thrilling Three to investigate, that
would be very helpful for my To-Do List. I

hoped they might just turn up, but to be
      honest it is all seeming a bit improbable.


Love from Pea xx

Then she started a new chapter of *The Adventures of Black-Eyed Pea.* She was just getting to a good bit, with sharks circling the pirate ship, when Tinkerbell's sleepy head dangled over the edge of the top bunk.

'Pea? You know ghosts?'

Pea put down her pen and peered upwards. 'Um. Not personally.'

'No, but . . . you know what I said about ghosts, to those boys? I was right, wasn't I? About them being stupid and made up?'

Pea sucked the end of her Special Writing Pen. She'd always prided herself on having quite a good imagination. She wanted to be a writer when she grew up, just like Mum, and that meant believing

**113**

in things. Coraly, one of Mum's Mermaid Girls from the books, was based on her, and she was a ghost now. It seemed rude not to believe in a character who was you, sort of.

'I don't know,' she said slowly. 'I've always thought . . .'

Suddenly Pea noticed that Tinkerbell's face looked pinched and anxious. Ghosts were supposed to come from dead people, after all.

'Of course you were right,' she said, in her most reassuringly big-sisterish voice. 'Ghosts are *totally* made up.'

'I knew it,' said Tinkerbell, flopping back into her bunk.

Pea tucked her owl notebook under her pillow, and clicked off the bedside lamp.

'Pea?'

'Yes, Tink?'

'What's hairy, bites people, and comes really close to you at the full moon?'

'Go to sleep, Tink.'

# CHAPTER 9

# THE THRILLING THREE

The next morning Pea went to the cupboard full of awful DVDs, collected all the jigsaws, and padlocked them into the garden shed (underneath the old wooden sledge, so Mum couldn't possibly find them again).

'It's my Neditorial duty,' she said sternly. Then she worried that she sounded a bit too Dreaded, so she promised to bring Mum a piece of carrot cake from the village bakery later as a treat if she wrote a whole new chapter. 'We'll be back at lunch time, and I want to see pages

**115**

and pages of new lovely pirates.'

'I won't delete a thing, I'll be ever so good,' promised Mum, fingers wiggling enthusiastically over her laptop.

'Fumes, fumes,' shouted Tinkerbell, making wafty motions with her hands as Pea dragged her out into the garden.

They left by the back gate, and walked across the common into the village. It was a big green space, littered with cowpats. Every now and then a little brown rabbit would dart out of the brambles round the edge, and Wuffly-Tim would spring after it, barking madly – which made the rabbit disappear again in a flash. They could see the castle ruins on the mound in the valley before them, grey clouds scooting overhead. There was a play park at the end of the common, with swings, a long peculiar sort of sliding bench with the head of a horse at one end, and an outdoor gym for grown-ups – but Tinkerbell turned up her nose at it.

'Investigating first, swings after.'

'Um. What are we investigating?' asked Pea anxiously.

'We're investigating where the nearest mystery is,' said Tinkerbell in a cross voice. 'Then, when we've found it, we can investigate that.'

They went to the shop, to look at the local paper for stories about escaped criminals, or sunken pirate ships. (There were none.) They checked the post office, in case there was a poster with MISSING SCIENTIST in the window. (There wasn't.)

Pea began to panic.

Then they went to the special Enid Blyton shop next door.

'Whoa,' said Tinkerbell softly.

The shop was small, dark and cosy, with racks and shelves piled high, and every inch of space filled up. There were rows and rows of books, and DVDs of the books, and birthday cards with the book covers on – even shiny helium balloons like the ones at birthday parties, with Enid Blyton's face printed on one side. There were old-fashioned games: cardboard planes to construct, or simple spinning tops and balls; and cellophane packets of wartime papers for you to fill in yourself – telegrams, and ration cards.

But Pea found herself transfixed by a display high up, on a shelf facing the door.

Golliwogs.

They were stiff, stuffed felt dolls with round black faces, bright red jackets and yellow bow ties. Pea had seen pictures of them before, at school. They'd done a lesson about them in History; how they had smiles and happy faces – but you shouldn't smile back when you saw one. They were dolls from a long time ago, in America, made by awful people who thought that having a black face – not one made of felt but a real one: a brown face made of skin – meant that you weren't as good as a white person.

She'd never seen one in a shop before. She wasn't even sure if it was a word you were supposed to say out loud; her skin went prickly and embarrassed even thinking about it. But there were lots of the dolls in the shop, in different sizes, next to a display of *Noddy* books – all written by Enid Blyton, with that same face on the cover.

Apparently Enid Blyton was 'bad' in more ways than even Dr Skidelsky had mentioned.

'I like those,' said Tinkerbell, pointing up at the dolls. 'We could get one for Dad, to sit by his bed in hospital.'

Pea didn't know what to say. Tinkerbell's face was brown. If she liked them, did that make them all right? She had no idea.

'Um. Let's look at the books first,' she murmured, steering Tinkerbell over to the other side of the shop.

Tinkerbell lingered at the bookshelves ('Read it, read it, reading it, read it . . .'), and did sums on her fingers to see what Clem's money would buy and still leave enough for fudge. In the end, to Pea's relief, she settled on one of the cellophane packets.

**119**

'We can send Dad a telegram,' she said. 'We did them in school – you just put in lots of STOPs and capital letters. I bet he'll be the only person in the hospital who gets one.'

When she paid, Tinkerbell asked the shop-keeper if she'd heard about any kidnappings lately – but the woman just laughed.

'Ha! She's going to feel pretty stupid when one happens,' said Tinkerbell, untying Wuffly from the railing outside the shop. 'Imagine being surr-ounded by books all about solving mysteries, and not noticing one right under your nose. Where next?'

'Um . . .' said Pea, feeling flustered. 'Maybe we could ask Eliza Hood, the archer? She works at the castle all day – if there's a mystery there, she might've seen some clues.'

But when they arrived at the castle gate, they found Ryan and Troy had got there first. They were in their PIE hoodies and sunglasses again, and were clearly on official PIE business: Ryan was inter-rogating a tall man dressed as a knight, videoing him with an iPad while Troy scanned him with his buzzy silver box. Pea spotted their dad's blue fisherman's hat a little further on. He was talking to the archer, and looked very serious and stern, now that he was awake.

Wuffly danced on her lead excitedly, but Tinkerbell pouted when she saw them. 'We'll come back later,' she muttered, turning away.

But it didn't help. For the rest of the morning it seemed that wherever they turned, there was PIE.

When they went den-hunting up the steep hill on the other side of the valley, they sat down to rest – and saw three black-clad figures halfway up the other slope, taking more videos of the castle.

When Pea went to buy ice creams, they were there in the queue. ('What does a sweaty ghost eat, Agent Ryan? Ice scream!' said Troy, hooting to himself. Pea smiled politely and wanted to say hello, but their huge dad was with them – he seemed even more huge up close – and she was too scared.)

And when they went to the bakery, there was a pile of printed flyers on the counter, with the green PIE logo in the corner.

## HAVE YOU SEEN THE GREY LADY?
### PROFESSIONAL GHOST HUNTERS PIE ARE IN THE AREA
### IF YOU HAVE EXPERIENCED A PARANORMAL EVENT
### PLEASE CONTACT:
**MAX MUNRO, CASTLE COTTAGE,**

**2 EAST STREET, CORFE CASTLE**

**WWW.PIEDINBURGH.CO.UK**

'Max Munro?' said Tinkerbell.

Pea guessed that must be the huge dad with the fisherman's hat. He must have helped them with the flyer, she thought; it looked very professional.

'We could make these!' said Tinkerbell, taking one. 'With a Thrilling Three logo on – when I've thought of one – asking people to tell us if they've got a mystery we can solve?'

Pea smiled with relief. That would keep Tinkerbell happily occupied for hours. And if someone else brought them a mystery, she could stop worrying about finding one.

She bought fresh bread for sandwiches and a Neditorial slice of carrot cake for Mum – but when they got home, they found her lying flat on the flowery sofa, watching one of the awful DVDs.

'I wrote a thrilling getaway, and two whole pages of very good pirate ship description!' she said, leaping up. 'Only then I got stuck trying to find new ways to describe the sea. *As blue as an eye, if you've got blue eyes,*' she read off the laptop screen, despair in her voice. 'And before that I had: *foamy, as if mermaids had been washing their hair in the bath.* Hopeless. But the pirate ship bit is good, my darling Neditor, I promise!'

On reading it, Pea declared that it was worth *half* a slice of cake – and Mum could look forward to the other half at the end of two more chapters, even if it took till tomorrow.

After lunch, Pea took the box of awful DVDs out of the cupboard, and padlocked that into the garden shed too.

Tinkerbell fetched the tent down from the bathroom, and they went into the garden to be undistracting. They didn't quite manage it (it is hard to be undistracting when shouting about the pointy end of poles being waved near people's eyes), but eventually the yellow tent was back up.

Tinkerbell found a broken-off slat of wood by the sledge in the shed. She wrote on it in marker pen, and balanced it proudly at the tent entrance.

DEN #2
Thrilling Three members only
No Trespassassers

'Why is it Den Number Two?' asked Pea, ignoring the spelling.

'Because it's only till we find a proper best den.'

Pea fetched their sleeping bags, and flowery cushions from the sofa to make the inside cosy ('Mum! Do I have to padlock the TV in the shed too?'), and all their colouring things and notebooks, and a pile of Enid Blytons. She fetched a packet of chocolate digestives too, for hungry emergencies, and tucked it into a secret pocket so Tinkerbell wouldn't eat them all at once.

Tinkerbell wrote Clem a telegram from the cellophane packet.

TO: DAD
FROM: US
BEST THING WE ARE THE THRILLING THREE
STOP WORST THING I HAVE NOT BOUGHT
FUDGE YET STOP I WILL THOUGH STOP

Then she started designing a Thrilling Three logo for their own flyer. Drawing a number three big enough to hold all the letters in 'Thrilling' involved a lot of rubbing-out and muttering, but eventually Tinkerbell sat back with a satisfied smile.

# MISTERY WANTED!

Has one of your family gone missing?
Is that person a spy or a scientist?
Or maybe you have lost a cat
or some treasure?

The Thrilling Three are mistery-solvers
(like the Famous Five, if you are sensible
people who know who the Famous Five are)

If you have any clues or if you are a kidnaper please tell us
we are at Rosebud Cottage, 32 East Street, Corfe Castle

P.S. NOT GHOSTS WE DO NOT HUNT THOSE

'Perfect,' said Pea.

If they were at home, they could've printed off lots of copies – but they had to make do with their best handwriting and felt-tip pens. They managed six before dinner. Once they were coloured in, the Thrilling Three logo was rather hard to read, and some of the spelling had become very creative – but Mum declared they had 'home-made charm'.

That night, after bedtime stories and tooth-brushing, Pea took out her To-Do List.

## PEA'S SUMMER HOLIDAY TO-DO LIST

Be a good Neditor for Mum

Give Tink a perfectly Famous Five holiday

Do all the things a Vitória would do
     (washing, shopping, tidying up, etc.)

Send Clem things to cheer him up

Mum was writing. Tinkerbell's mystery was on its way. Teeth had been brushed, and Clem's telegram would be posted tomorrow.

She crept downstairs, opened the fridge, and bit off a small morsel of Mum's half-slice of carrot cake; just a tiny corner. Then gave herself a sticker – an orang-utan with its thumbs up, saying GOOD JOB!

'Good job,' she whispered.

Then she went to brush her teeth again.

# CHAPTER
# 10

# SALTY JAKE

**Sunday 26 July**

Dear Diary,
Tink has invented a Thrilling Three uniform. It
is pyjama bottoms, a bobble hat, an orange
number three made of cardboard and a
safety pin, and a belt made from sticky tape
for holding equipment: torch, pencil case,
Enid Blyton book. She wore it all round the
village when we gave out our flyers. (I just

wore the orange number three on my jumper.)

We saw PIE. They stared at us. (I think. It is hard to know with sunglasses.)

Mum spent all morning making a huge pirate ship out of Post-it notes.

I have locked the Post-it notes in the shed.

No one has replied to our Thrilling Three advert yet, but I am trying to be patient (even though Tinkerbell says being patient is Anne-ish).

Stickers earned by Mum: none.
Stickers earned by me: none.

## Monday 27 July

Dear Diary,
Brilliant day! Mum found a box of CDs and some big headphones in the cupboard. It turns out

that *Ocean Sounds Volume II* is very good pirate-writing music.

Clover phoned to say she has auditions tomorrow for the Cheseman Hall theatre camp big production of *Peter Pan*. Apparently very important agents and people come to watch and do 'talent-spotting', so she needs a new stage name that is as memorable as Edison Hackleback. (That's what Agata's going to be called if she gets famous.) I don't think Edison Hackleback sounds like a name at all, but Clover says that's why it's so unforgettable. Me and Tinkerbell texted her a list:

Clover-Jane Sticklebrick
Smith-Anne Magillycuddy
Anderson Jack
Branderson Black
Harpsichord Hop-Scotcherson
Gruffalo Jones
Banana Pencil
Envelope Toastcrumb

The last ones were just Tinkerbell naming things that were on the table, but actually Envelope Toastcrumb is my favourite. (You say Envelope like 'Penelope'.)

No one has replied to our advert again.

Stickers earned by Mum: one.
Stickers earned by me: one.

=====================================

**Tuesday 28 July**

Dear Diary,
I think the Blyton fumes have stopped working. *Ocean Sounds Volume II* is very good pirate-writing music, but it turns out that *Ocean Sounds Volume III* is soothing swishy noises designed to help you go to sleep. Mum spent all afternoon snoring. Now Dr Skidelsky's laptop has dribble on it and Mum has keyboardface and no new words.

I lent Mum my Special Writing Pen, but she just stares at the owl floating up and down so I have hidden it under my pillow.

For dinner I invented pirate soup, to be inspiring. Pirate soup is tomato soup out of a tin with blue food colouring in it to make it like the sea, and boats made of potato wedges with lettuce sails. All the boats sank. I don't think I'm going to invent soup again.

Tinkerbell has started a new book called *Five Sit Around Being Bored Because Nothing Fun Ever Happens in Dorset*. I hope she doesn't send it to Clem – he was already a bit confused by her telegram.

No one has answered our advert. I am beginning to think that 'home-made charm' is not what kidnappers, missing scientists, etc., like best.

Tinkerbell was obviously thinking it too. Pea found her in the tent the next day, clutching the fancy printed PIE flyer and trying to draw a new version of the Thrilling Three logo.

'I wish Sam One was here,' she sighed, rubbing out her fifth attempt.

Pea wished he was too. He'd sent another postcard – *They made me go on a horse. I didn't like it*, it said – and Pea had sent one back, with a photo of the castle on the front, but it wasn't the same. She missed having someone to talk to. Not that Tinkerbell wasn't fun – but it wasn't the same as having someone to share worries with; a friend who she would always look after, but who would look after her back.

She missed Clover too.

Tiptoeing up to the bedroom so no one could hear, Pea took out the mobile phone and called her.

'It's Pea. How did your audition go?'

Clover coughed. 'I don't know. They wouldn't

let me use any of your clever new names, because I was already Clover on their big list, and . . . I'm not sure if . . . they haven't told us what parts we've got yet, that's all. Obviously the audition went completely wonderfully!'

Her voice went squeaky, like a nervous mouse – but she insisted she was *entirely* well and *utterly* cheerful, and longing to hear all their news.

'Mum's book is doing lots better,' Pea whispered. 'But I don't know what to do about Tink. I think she's starting to hate the Famous Five. We've been here for nearly a whole week and we *still* haven't found a kidnapped scientist or a sinister criminal.'

'Oh. Were you expecting to?'

'Yes! Well, a bit.'

'Silly Pea. Real life isn't like in stories. Sometimes it's quite sad and disappointing and terribly unfair.'

Usually when Clover called her silly, it wasn't

all that welcome – but at that moment Pea found it oddly reassuring. It wasn't her fault at all; it was just real life, being not like a book.

'But what do I do? I promised Clem.'

There was a silence while Clover thought. 'You're good at stories. Can't you make one up?'

'Like . . . a treasure map? Or a secret code?'

'Exactly! Something with a bit of drama, to remind Tink why she liked doing Famous Five things in the first place. Oh, I wish I was there to help. Are you sure you don't need me?'

Pea looked at the copy of *Five on a Hike Together* lying on Tinkerbell's pillow, and smiled. She knew at once what to do, and she very much needed Clover's help – or at least her voice.

They spent a long time whispering and making a plan.

That night, Pea arranged a special picnic tea in the tent – 'so Mum can keep on writing without any disturbingness' – and promised to play any game Tinkerbell wanted, for at least an hour.

If Tinkerbell noticed Pea anxiously checking her watch every few minutes, she didn't say anything.

At exactly 6.29 p.m., Pea took a very deep breath.

'Whatever's that?' she said, jerking her head up sharply as if there had been a very loud noise outside.

'I can't hear anything,' said Tinkerbell.

Pea slipped outside for a moment, her heart thumping unsteadily in her chest, then came back. 'How funny, I must've imagined it,' she said, in a rather unnatural voice.

A moment later, there was an odd rustling outside, and the sound of coughing, coming from the garden gate.

'Oi! Billybob!' hissed a sinister voice.

Tinkerbell's eyes went wide. She clutched Wuffly tightly.

Pea put her finger to her lips, so they could listen.

'Billybob, you there?' said the voice again. It sounded like a croaky old woman. 'Salty Jake's changed the plan. Nessie's cave, midnight on Tuesday. That's where you'll find the goods.'

Tinkerbell's mouth fell open.

There was another lot of rustling, then the voice fell silent.

They scrambled out of the tent and ran to the gate – but there was no one to be seen. Tinkerbell opened the gate and peered up and down the common, but the creaky-voiced old crone had vanished. All that was left was a set of very clear footprints in the mud by the gate, one a small shoe-print, the other a circle – as if whoever had whispered over the gate had a wooden leg.

'Wow!' said Tinkerbell, beaming fit to burst. 'Pirate footprints! And a secret message! Sniff the trail, Wuffly-Tim – maybe they've left a scent behind on an old handkerchief. No? That's very mysterious. Let me get the camera – I've got

**138**

to take a photo of these footprints! Woo-hoo! The Thrilling Three have a mystery to solve!'

She went zipping off into the house – leaving Pea plenty of time to reach into the bushes by the gatepost and pick up the mobile phone. She switched off the speakerphone, whispered a quick, 'Thank you, Clover, that was perfect!' then hung up and slipped it into her pocket. She made sure the shoe (one of Mum's) and the broom handle she'd used to make the wooden leg print were safely hidden away too.

Wuffly watched all this solemnly, blinking up at Pea with her big brown eyes in a way that made her feel slightly guilty – but when Tinkerbell hurried up to bed early, with a Blyton book in one hand and the secret message in the other, sticky-tape belt in place, she felt very proud of herself.

It was just like being Enid Blyton, Pea thought – only without any of the bits Dr Skidelsky wouldn't like.

Dear Clem,

Everything is going brilliantly! Please don't
worry if you get telegrams from Tinkerbell
about caves, smugglers, etc. I am just being an
excellent big sister.

I hope you're feeling a bit better. We miss you!

Love from Pea xx

---

Dear Enid Blyton,

I know people say your books are too simple
and silly, but I think you are a very confusing
writer. Usually I just love things or don't like
them at all, e.g. Marmite sandwiches. But with
you it is both at once.

I wish you hadn't put things like those dolls

in your Noddy books or made Anne do all the washing-up. But thank you for the good bits, because they make my little sister very happy.

I hope I'm allowed to like things when not all of them is perfect.

Love from Pea xx

The proud feeling didn't last.

For one thing, she hadn't planned what Clover was going to say carefully enough. She woke up to find Tinkerbell testing every clock in the house, to see if it had an alarm that would wake her up in time for midnight on Tuesday. And while 'Nessie's Cave' had sounded wonderfully mysterious, there was no such place.

'There's lots of other caves near here,' said Tinkerbell, spreading out a map she'd found on the cottage bookshelf.

There were, too: real caves, and harbours. Tinkerbell also found a book all about smugglers in Dorset, filled with tales of secret sunken tubs of treasure, hidden underwater then brought ashore by boat, or tucked away inside a maze of tunnels and caves. She marked all the caves and harbours on the map with Post-it notes from the shed: Tilly Whim, Winspit, Dancing Ledge, Durlston Head and Lulworth Cove.

It all sounded so perfectly Blyton-ish, Pea began to wish Salty Jake and his 'goods' *were* real. It wasn't anything like as much fun as solving a real mystery – not for Pea, who knew there wasn't an answer. Besides, they couldn't go sailing off in a little boat to search for sunken treasure. Most of the caves were incredibly hard to reach, and no one was allowed inside in case of rock falls or dangerous tides.

'I'm really small – I could fit in a cave without there being rock falls,' said Tinkerbell, with alarming confidence.

Pea began to wish she'd never invented Salty Jake.

She took Mum a fresh mug of Special Writing Tea, and hovered till there was a pause in her typing.

'Mum? You know when you're writing, and you make up a bit of plot, and then it turns out that another bit of plot would be better . . . What happens?'

Mum smiled. 'I just go back and change it. You know I had Janet the pirate stow away by hiding in a basket of laundry? She doesn't any more. Now she's wrapped up inside the topsail – so when *The Maggot* sets sail, it all unfurls and she falls out onto the deck. It's a much better scene. That's why writing's easier than real life: if you don't like how things are going, you cross out the bad bits and start again.'

Pea smiled weakly, then tiptoed up to the bedroom to call Clover again. But her emergency mobile number just rang and rang, with no answer.

Pea had to leave a message: 'It's all gone wrong, Clover! I need you to call back and say, *Never mind, Salty Jake's already picked up the goods!* in your best croaky old crone voice, otherwise Tinkerbell will be crushed by rocks, and it'll all be our fault.'

There was a little whimper from outside.

Pea froze.

Wuffly padded into the room and laid her nose on Pea's knee – followed a moment later by Tinkerbell, her eyes huge and shiny.

'You mean . . . Salty Jake isn't real?' she whispered.

# CHAPTER 11

# JAMPIRES AND NOT-GINGER BEER

Pea felt dreadful.

It didn't matter how many times she explained to Tinkerbell that she had only invented Salty Jake and Nessie's Cave to be kind. It had still been a lie, and no one likes to be lied to.

Tinkerbell lay on her top bunk and cried. She tore up her orange Thrilling Three badge.

She scribbled on her half-finished *Five Meet the Thrilling Three and Catch Salty Jake* book cover.

At dinner time, Pea wrote out a menu with

all Tinkerbell's favourite things: Pot Noodle, and volcano toasties with cheese and baked beans, and bottles of not-ginger beer (lemonade) with a twirly straw stuck in the neck – but Tinkerbell scrumpled it up.

Clover still wouldn't answer her phone. Pea couldn't call Clem. And Mum was no help: Pea peeked into the living room, but she was typing frantically with one hand and clutching a large mug of black coffee with the other, headphones on and a fast tinny beat pulsing from them. She was still there when they went to bed.

Tinkerbell put her fingers in her ears when Pea read her a bedtime story, but she kept going anyway. It made her feel less lonely, to hear the sound of her own voice reading out loud.

'You can't stay cross with me for ever,' she said when Tinkerbell greeted her morning bowl of cereal with a sulk. 'Or . . . well, yes, you probably could. But it's only Friday, Tink. Don't spoil it. It's not going to make Clem feel better if you

**146**

send him telegrams about how horrible your holiday is.'

'No more lying?'

'No more lying. None at all.'

The sulk faded, ever so slightly.

Pea got Tinkerbell to write a list of fun things she'd like to do.

Solve a real mistery

Eat cake

Go to the play park

Go to the castle (inside it properly, with tickets)

Pea said, very gently, that she couldn't promise to make all of those things happen, not without lying – but they could definitely do the cake and the play park bit straight away, and she would do her very best with the rest.

They left Mum a note (speedy typing was already coming from behind the living-room door, which

Pea felt a good Neditor would never interrupt), and set off with Wuffly across the common.

The swings and the horse-faced slidy-bench were fairly dull, but to Pea's relief Tinkerbell's tired face and red-rimmed eyes soon changed when they went to the outdoor gym. They tested out all the machines – in case, Tinkerbell explained, the Thrilling Three needed to chase after villains or climb up any ropes. (Wuffly mainly ran in a circle barking, but since Timmy in the books did that quite often, it felt like it might be valuable training.)

Then they went to the Castle Tea Rooms, for cake. Pea sent Tinkerbell to claim a table for them while she waited in the long queue to order.

She was just wondering if ginger beer might taste nicer the second time you tried it when there was a crackle of static.

'Agent Ryan?' came a muffled, disembodied Scottish voice through a walkie-talkie. 'Agent Ryan, please respond. One of those weirdo UHES

**148**

we met on the bridge has come to sit on the table next to me. She appears to be hostile and is armed with a hairy beast, which I suspect may be part-werewolf. What should I do? Over.'

Standing directly ahead of her in the queue was Ryan, fumbling with his walkie-talkie. Pea peered through the crowds and spotted Tinkerbell, arms folded protectively around Wuffly, eyes at maximum glare, staring at Troy, who was sitting at the next-door table.

'Remain in position, Agent Troy. Over and out,' hissed Ryan, before shoving the walkie-talkie back into his belt.

There was a long uncomfortable pause.

Pea was sure he must know she was behind him, and had heard – but he didn't say anything.

'Um,' said Pea eventually. 'Sorry about Tinkerbell. She's a bit upset so she's extra fierce today, but she's nice really. Well, nice-ish.'

Ryan still said nothing.

Pea didn't much like talking to strangers, either,

but she thought he was being quite rude now. Did he never make friends with people who didn't believe in ghosts – or was it just her?

'Um,' said Pea again. 'Hello?'

Ryan turned round, lowered his sunglasses, and said quietly, 'No offence, but I'm not interested in a girlfriend.'

Pea laughed. Then she put her hand over her mouth, in case she was the one being rude. This wasn't the sort of thing Enid Blyton had prepared her for.

'I'm not interested in a boyfriend, either. I was just being friendly.' She hesitated. 'Being a girl doesn't mean I want to be someone's girlfriend. My sister's not being your brother's girlfriend just because they're talking. Or, um, hitting each other. Tink! Tink, let go of his hair!'

She flapped her hand frantically across the crowded tea rooms, until Tinkerbell released Troy from her grip. They both sat back down, edging their chairs further apart and sulking.

Ryan frowned at Pea. 'That girl can't be your sister.'

This, at least, Pea was prepared for. She affected a weary yawn, learned from Clover specifically for whenever this question arose.

'Now you're just being ignorant. All families are different. Me and Tinkerbell don't look the same, but it doesn't make us any less sisterish.'

She folded her arms sternly, ready to argue. But Ryan shuffled awkwardly, and she remembered his limp and his hand. Ryan and Troy didn't look the same either.

'Oh! I didn't mean . . . I wasn't . . .' she said quickly.

'You're fine,' said Ryan, just as quickly. 'Fair point. I apologize.'

'Oh. Good. Thanks.'

At that moment Ryan got to the front of the queue, and had to step away to give his order. Pea wasn't sure which of them was more relieved.

It was rather awkward, sitting next to the PIE

**151**

boys in the busy, noisy tea rooms, pretending they weren't there, in their sunglasses and matching uniforms. Tinkerbell took out her book. Pea started writing in her owl notebook – but neither of them was really concentrating.

'What's got fangs, sleeps in a coffin, and is chock full of raspberries?' said Troy.

'A jampire,' said Ryan, in a weary voice.

Pea giggled, until Tinkerbell kicked her under the table.

'What's got fangs, sleeps in a coffin, and gives you socks for Christmas?'

'A grampire,' said Ryan, just as wearily.

Pea pressed her lips together tightly.

'What's got fangs, sleeps in a coffin, and goes Oink?'

'A hampire,' sighed Ryan.

That time even Tinkerbell smiled, though she put her book up over her mouth so the boys wouldn't see.

Pea tried very hard to think of something that

rhymed with vampire so she could join in, but all she could think of was: *What's got fangs, sleeps in a coffin, and lives next door to us? A Sampire* – which Sam One would've found very funny, but the PIE boys wouldn't understand at all.

She reminded herself that it didn't matter, them not wanting to be friends. The Thrilling Three could still have fun. She could find them a mystery without making one up – and without needing a fancy flyer or a proper logo. But then the waiter brought over their orders: two huge slabs of chocolate cake for the boys, plus posh hot chocolates with marshmallows and cream, while Pea had only ordered one scone and one not-ginger beer with two straws, to share. When Ryan and Troy both took out iPads and started to watch ghost videos over and over again, Pea found herself feeling ever so slightly second-best.

To judge by Tinkerbell's gloomy slurping – all performed with huge eyes locked enviously on Troy's iPad screen – she felt the same. Even Wuffly looked glum, her head resting on Tinkerbell's knee, her tail drooping.

Eventually, once every last crumb of scone was gone, Pea sent Tinkerbell out to let Wuffly run around.

The waiter brought their bills, and Pea poked through her red spotty purse for the right money, feeling extra grown up as she added extra coins for a tip. Ryan sent Troy outside but he still made no move to pay their bill. He just sat there, very stiffly, eyes hidden by his sunglasses, tinkering with the video still playing on his iPad – though he didn't seem to be watching it.

He went on sitting there.

Pea didn't know what to do. She knew nothing about people with a stiff arm who walked a bit unusually; might he suddenly have got worse, or need some help? Mum had said to ask him, but she wasn't sure how. She looked around for a suitable grown-up sort of person for help – and that was when she noticed that the PIE boys were out by themselves. Their huge dad, in his funny fisherman's hat, was, for once, nowhere to be seen.

She looked at the red flush creeping up Ryan's neck. This wasn't anything to do with his arm or his leg, she realized.

'Um,' she said, in a low voice. 'Did you forget your wallet or something? It's OK – I can lend you some money.'

Ryan made a strange huffing noise, as if he'd been holding in a breath and suddenly didn't have to.

'My dad usually pays,' he hissed. 'Only I kind of asked him not to come along with us for a wee while, you know? And I don't . . . he'll think . . .'

Their dad did look quite scary, Pea thought; he was probably the shouty cross sort. She smiled. 'It's OK. I understand.'

She read their bill, then took out some of Clem's money and put the right amount on the table.

Tinkerbell poked her nose back into the tea rooms. 'Pea! Come on! Stop talking to the enemy!'

**155**

'I'll pay you back, I swear it,' Ryan whispered.

But Pea's eyes were fixed on the iPad. Ryan had left a video running on a loop: a ghostly greyish face hovering in a high window of the castle, turning to look at the camera, then darting quickly away as if trying to hide.

'But that's . . .' she murmured.

'Thought you didn't believe in ghosts?' said Ryan, relaxing enough to give her a little smirk. 'There's proof you're wrong. That's the Grey Lady – or her missing head, anyway.'

Pea shook her head slowly, hardly believing what she was seeing. A face framed by neat dark curls, a string of pearls, a soft serious smile.

'That's not the Grey Lady,' she said, breathlessly. 'That's the ghost of *Enid Blyton*.'

# TO THE CASTLE!

They all sat on the stone memorial in the middle of the village square.

'You think Corfe Castle's being haunted by *Enid Blyton*?' said Tinkerbell, her voice full of wonder.

'By her head, anyway,' said Pea. '*Look.*'

They gathered around the iPad to watch the video again. There it was: that softly smiling face, floating quite without a body, peeping eerily out at them – then suddenly ducking out of view.

Tinkerbell opened the back page of her book to show the photograph of Blyton inside, holding them up to compare.

'Whoa,' she said. 'It really *is* her!'

'Who is she again?' said Troy, taking off his sunglasses so he could see better.

Tinkerbell rolled her eyes and explained about ginger beer, and hundreds of books.

'So – did Enid Blyton ever get beheaded?'

'No!' said Pea. Then she hesitated. She didn't know for definite – but she thought it was the sort of thing that a website would mention. And the *Famous Five* books were old, but not as old as the Grey Lady; people didn't get be-headed by the time they were written. 'This doesn't make any sense. Hasn't the Grey Lady been haunting the castle since the English Civil War? Enid Blyton wasn't alive then. Anyway, isn't the Grey Lady meant to be headless?'

Ryan shrugged one shoulder. 'Thousand-year-old castles often attract more than one spirit. Our Grey Lady's still out there too, I reckon.'

Tinkerbell's eyes went wide. 'Wow. Do you

think her and Enid Blyton get together and have ghost adventures?'

'Thought you didn't believe in ghosts?' said Troy, grinning as Wuffly nuzzled his hands.

Tinkerbell bit her lip and looked at Pea, plainly torn.

Pea blinked. 'I don't know,' she whispered. 'I didn't . . . but, well. She's definitely dead, and that is *definitely* her.'

The video was still replaying on Ryan's iPad, that eerie ghostly face turning away again and again. Pea had a lurking feeling that there was something not quite right about what she was seeing; as if the perfect soft smile and string of pearls was a clue, in some way. But there was no denying whose face it was.

A thrill ran down her spine. She had written that letter, asking Enid Blyton for help with Mum's book. Even if she hadn't sent it anywhere, had that brought her back? Was she *their* ghost, personally arriving to deliver Blyton fumes?

'I think I *want* to believe . . .' she said slowly.

'Me too,' said Tinkerbell at once, nodding rapidly as if Pea had given her some sort of permission.

'But I'd like to investigate it properly,' Pea went on.

'Aye, we're on it,' said Ryan. 'EMF readings, spectrum analysis – and now we've got a possible ID, we can start cross-referencing other sightings, looking for bio-clues . . .'

Pea coughed. 'Um. I just meant – we should go to the castle. To that window. Where the ghost is.'

Ryan and Troy exchanged sighs.

'It's a haunting,' said Ryan. 'A spirit? You don't just . . . go to it.'

'Why not?' said Tinkerbell.

The boys didn't seem to have an answer for that.

'The Thrilling Three for ever!' Tinkerbell yelled, running towards the path across the common.

'We'll come and tell you if we find anything,' Pea shouted over her shoulder.

They raced home. Even Wuffly didn't bother to chase the rabbits.

'Mum! Mum, we have to go to the castle, we have to go *now*!' yelled Tinkerbell, grabbing her bobble-hat, and starting to sticky-tape all her equipment round her tummy.

'We do, we really do – your Neditor says so,' Pea added breathlessly. 'Oh! Are you all right? You're a bit . . . stinky.'

Mum was slumped in her chair, still in yesterday's clothes, groaning.

'No coffee for me, ever again,' she moaned, rubbing her eyes. 'I thought it would keep me awake and alert and brimming with good ideas, and it did, all yesterday – but then I felt so awake I thought I might as well keep writing all night, and . . . oh dear. I'm not sure three o'clock in the morning words are as good as daytime ones. It looks like I've invented a new sort of poisonous sea spider called a Pig-nosed Tormentula. Is that good? I can't tell any more.'

Pea packed Mum off to wash while she read the new chapters out loud to Tinkerbell, who oohed and eeked in all the right places, and looked positively cross when it stopped in the middle of a sentence. There were twenty whole pages of good ideas and clever writing, and an exciting bit where Janet the pirate kicked her way out of the rum barrel she'd been nailed into, and leaped off Rebecca Blackheart's ship *into the bleak black seas beneath* – only to find herself swimming through a hairy-legged pod of tormentulas, puffing out poison in inky purple clouds.

'Three-o'clock-in-the-morning words are the *best*,' Tinkerbell declared when Mum emerged from the shower. 'You should probably never go to sleep again.'

'Really?' Mum smiled, more happily than Pea had seen all holiday. 'Right then, my hens – I'm having the rest of the day off. The castle it is!'

*

Eliza the archer was at the castle gates again, welcoming visitors with a slap of her thigh and the offer to pose for a photo.

'Welcome, good ladies, welcome all!' she said, bowing deeply as Wuffly snuffled at her leather boots.

They marched up the long sloping path, through the gatehouse, and inside at last.

At once Pea was hit by a waft of woodsmoke and wet dog and hay, a welcoming homey sort of smell. There were tents dotted all around the flat ground below the castle, though not like their yellow one; these were white canvas, with pointy wooden poles sticking out of the tops, and thick guy ropes.

There was an apothecary – like a doctor, with a string of smelly dried herbs.

There was an archery display, with two people in floaty white shirts like Eliza's firing longbows into a wicker target.

A sword-fighting school . . . a dressing-up room

where you could have your picture taken in medieval outfits . . . a crackling fire with a blacksmith, hammering horseshoes and cooking bacon in a huge blackened frying pan . . .

Pea only had eyes for the castle. There was the same magical thrum in the air that she'd felt when they'd first walked into the village, hoping to go in; a thrilling feeling that something amazing might be about to happen.

Blyton fumes, wafting through the air.

Did that mean the ghost was nearby? Was Enid Blyton herself watching over them? Were they about to meet her ghost, up there in the tower?

No wonder Mum's writing was suddenly going so brilliantly.

'You're very quiet, Pea,' said Mum.

(There had been an extra emergency meeting of the Thrilling Three at the garden gate, to decide whether to tell Mum about the Blyton ghost – but they had agreed it should stay their secret, in case it distracted her from inspiring piratical thoughts.)

'I'm just excited,' whispered Pea.

Mum made for the dressing-up tent, but Pea and Tinkerbell gripped one elbow each, and marched her up the hill.

Now that they were actually inside, the castle seemed enormous. They passed through a second gatehouse with more rooms; ones you could duck down and walk into, with crumbled staircases leading to nowhere.

Mum lingered, running her hands over the aged stone. 'Gosh. Maybe once the *Pirate Girls* are done, I might have to think about *Castle Girls*. Or *Medieval Girls*?' She peered through an arrow slit. 'There could be an outlaw who loved archery, and one who was an apprentice blacksmith, and maybe a noble princess one who wasn't meant to talk to the others so it had to be a secret . . .'

Pea liked the sound of that very much (so long as one of them was like Coraly, and looked like her) – but there was no time to think about that now.

'Come *on*,' said Tinkerbell, pushing Mum through the old stone doorway and on up the hill.

Pea squinted, her hair blowing into her eyes as they rose higher, the path winding up the mound. The castle was an utter ruin, with only one vast wall still standing – but there were wooden steps and walkways up to allow you to enter two rooms high up, with square windows.

'Up there – that's where she was!' whispered Tinkerbell, tugging Pea's sleeve.

They dashed up the wooden steps, dodging a stone room marked GARDEROBE ('That's medieval for *toilet* – yuck,' said Tinkerbell, reading the sign and wrinkling her nose). Pea waited breathlessly for some other visitors to go past, then stepped out of the sunshine and into the passageway.

Here it was cool and dark. There was damp mossy stone all around. Two empty doorways faced her, marked SOUTH KEEP on a metal plaque. Pea ignored the first, and went straight to the second doorway, her heart in her mouth.

She felt a moment's panic. Did she really want to meet a floating head, even if it belonged to Enid Blyton? Did she really want to see a ghost up close?

'What's that?'

Tinkerbell stepped in front of her, Wuffly tangling around her ankles, and pointed up.

Inside the small stone room, high above the square window, something dangled – something silver, tied with a string that was caught between two jutting chunks of stone. The silver thing looked a bit like a jellyfish: puffy, with one domed side. It blew about, darting in front of the window from time to time.

Suddenly there was an especially powerful gust of wind – and the silver thing came free of the string, and floated up into the air.

'Catch it!' yelled Tinkerbell.

The silver jellyfish hovered, terrifyingly, on the lip of the window.

Pea lunged forward – reached out with both

hands – and clutched the jellyfish tight. She half expected it to melt into nothing in her fingers, but instead her hands sank into some sort of crunchy plastic.

'Oh! It's a balloon, isn't it?' said Mum. 'One of those helium ones you get at birthday parties.'

With a sinking heart, Pea turned it over.

It *was* a balloon, but not from a birthday party.

A silver balloon from the shop in the village square, printed with the softly smiling face of Enid Blyton.

# CHAPTER 13

# UNPROOF

Ryan and Troy's front door was red like the Llewellyns' one at home – but tomato, rather than raspberry.

'Are you sure this is the right place?' said Mum as Pea reached up to ring the bell. 'And these boys won't mind you just turning up on their doorstep to give them a manky old balloon?'

Tinkerbell thrust the PIE leaflet under her nose. 'Look! Castle Cottage, East Street. Max Munro: that's their dad. They *want* us to bring them ghost information and stuff.'

Pea held the squashy balloon tight in her arms,

and fretted. She felt disappointed, and she'd only started believing in ghosts that morning. She wasn't at all sure they'd welcome *this* sort of information.

When the boys' father pulled open the door, his big tall body filled up the whole doorway. Pea's courage failed, and she tucked herself behind Mum, and let her do the talking.

'Hello there,' said Mum brightly. 'This probably sounds bonkers, but apparently we're looking for PIE?'

'We're here to see Agent Ryan and Agent Troy,' said Tinkerbell.

'Then you're in the right place,' he said, in the same familiar accent as the boys', but much, much deeper. 'Come in, come in. My boys have found themselves a pair of wee girlfriends, eh?'

Pea winced. It had been a bit annoying when Ryan said it, but they'd sorted it out. Now here she was having to explain that she was just a person all over again – when Max was a grown-up, and new, and ever so slightly scary.

'A pair of investigators, I think they'd call themselves,' Mum said swiftly, stroking Pea's ponytail. 'I'm so pleased they've been making friends while I've been chained to my desk – and, well, goodness knows, I could do with a little adult conversation. I'm Bree – this is Pea, and Tinkerbell. Oh, and this is Wuffly, but I can take her away if you aren't doggy people.'

'Max Munro, Paranormal Investigations Edinburgh,' he said, shaking her hand and welcoming them inside. 'And these are my two: Ryan and Troy – Troy's doggy people, for sure. They've got one back at home – lives with their mother. So, Bree, it's a working holiday for you too, eh?'

Pea tiptoed inside. Tinkerbell followed, clutching Wuffly's lead possessively.

Castle Cottage was much grander than their own. The whole ground floor was all one room, with massive leather sofas and a very shiny kitchen at the back. There was a huge fireplace, and some of the walls still showed the original bumpy stones,

**171**

but it didn't feel old-fashioned at all; there was pale grey carpet under their feet, and a giant TV screen hung above the fire.

Mum and Max sat down and began having one of *those* conversations, all about weather and traffic jams.

The Thrilling Three and PIE sat in awkward silence on opposite sides of the room. The boys put on their sunglasses and folded their arms. Tinkerbell suddenly looked self-conscious in her bobble-hat and sticky-tape belt.

'Why should you never play hide-and-seek with a ghost's mum and dad?' said Troy eventually.

'Not now, Agent Troy,' said Ryan. He nodded at Pea. 'What *is* that?'

Pea held the squashy balloon on her lap, like a deflated silver cat. Reluctantly, she explained where they had found it.

'What?' said Mum, overhearing. 'Why would you think Enid Blyton was haunting the castle?'

Ryan picked up one of the iPads, and showed her the video.

'I did wonder why her face was so exactly the same as the one in the photograph,' said Pea miserably. 'But . . . I still quite wanted it to be real.'

'Oh, but it's perfect!' said Mum, clapping her hands. 'It's just like one of the *Famous Five* stories! You know, they see a spooky face, they investigate, and it turns out to be smugglers!'

Pea looked mournfully at the balloon. 'But it isn't smugglers *or* a ghost. It's a balloon.'

'So now *nobody* wins,' said Tinkerbell.

'Rubbish! You still solved the mystery. I think Enid Blyton herself would be impressed.'

Tinkerbell looked more hopeful, but Pea wasn't so sure, especially when Max leaned in, fixing her with a very serious expression.

'You know, Pea, virtually all ghost sightings turn out to have a natural explanation,' he said. 'It's just that usually there's nothing to prove it one way or another; only whether you believe or not.

With this castle ghost of yours – well, you've got concrete evidence. Not proof of a ghostly presence, granted. More like . . . unproof. Which still has value, because now no one will waste time trying to find that particular ghost again. Do you follow?'

He leaned in close, a keen spark in his eyes. Pea looked at his fuzzy beard and his round tummy, and thought that he wasn't really how she'd imagined him at all: not severe, or scary; more like a very intense teddy bear.

'So – you don't mind that it's not really a ghost?'

Ryan shook his head. 'We're used to it. We'd get loads more hits on the website if we put up a balloon with a face on it than we would for one without an explanation. Dad says it makes people feel clever, if they know what really happened. Like the Feejee Mermaid.'

Pea and Tinkerbell both gazed blankly at Mum.

'Don't look at me. My mermaids are all made up.'

'So's this one,' said Max. 'Hand me that book,

will you, Pea? The one with the Loch Ness Monster on the cover?'

There was a neat pile of books on the coffee table nearest to Pea. *100 Paranormal Mysteries Explained!* was sitting on the top. Max flipped through the pages, then laid the book flat so they could all see.

*The Feejee Mermaid Hoax*, said the heading. Below was a black-and-white drawing of a shrivelled-up creature with a huge head and a fishy tail.

'Yuck,' said Tinkerbell. 'That's not a mermaid!'

'Quite right,' said Max. 'It's a dead monkey and an old fish sewn together. But people believed it was the real thing for years – because they wanted to.'

Pea leaned closer to read. Apparently there were lots of Feejee mermaids, made up to fool people. The one in the picture was put in a glass case and shown at a fair in America in 1842 – and huge crowds lined up to see it. Knowing that, she felt a lot less daft for imagining that a balloon was a ghost.

'Of course, finding proof of a *real* mermaid – now that would be the ultimate,' said Max, with a sigh.

'Ha, I can imagine!' said Mum, laughing. Then she coughed, suddenly awkward as she glanced between Max and the boys, properly taking in their hoodies and the piles of books. 'Sorry. I didn't realize you really meant . . . I mean – it's only stories, isn't it? Sirens luring ships onto the rocks . . . that's just a pretty excuse for not being very good at steering your ship.'

'Maybe,' said Max. 'Maybe not. Mermaids show up all over the world – in art, carvings, whatever – all through history. Think about it. What's more likely: that artists thousands of miles or thousands of years apart drew mermaids out of their imaginations, or that they drew a thing they'd actually seen?'

'Whoa . . .' breathed Tinkerbell.

Pea hadn't met many grown-up men who didn't roll their eyes at the mention of mermaids, and no boys at all; even Sam One was wary. But Ryan and Troy didn't giggle, or laugh. Ryan fetched the iPad, and showed them stories of cruel serpent-tailed Russian Rusalki, of kindly Greek Nereids, of Nigerian Mami Watas who took drowned spirits to another world (and only sometimes brought them back) – talking about each with that same intense interest as his dad. The more he spoke, the more Pea felt herself swept along, wanting to believe too.

'Maybe we should add mermaid-hunting to our schedule, eh, lads?' said Max.

'No way!' said Troy. 'We go home at the end of next week – and so far all we've got is a photo of ectoplasm that some old woman put through our letter box.'

'Ectoplasm?' asked Mum.

'Goo,' said Troy happily. 'Like ghost snot.'

'How many times, Troy! It's not snot!' Ryan sighed heavily. 'It's this stuff that spirit activity sometimes leaves behind. We were hoping it might give us a starting point for tracking the ghost, but, uh . . .' He lowered his voice. 'Actually I think she's given us a photo of a slug somebody squished. They do look kind of similar.'

Tinkerbell giggled.

Pea grinned, then caught Mum's eye. She was watching them thoughtfully.

'You know, Ryan, Troy,' she said, 'these two only started looking for Enid today and they've already found her. If I was trying to hunt down a ghost, I'd want them on my team.'

'*Mu-um,*' hissed Tinkerbell, hiding her face in Wuffly's hair.

'Oh, all right, I am a bit biased. And a teeny bit keen to get rid of you, to be honest, my lambs, so that I can get on with my book. That's if Max really meant what he said earlier, about taking you off my hands a few days this week? You weren't just offering to be polite?'

Max twinkled. 'Not at all – would be a pleasure.

OK, lads?'

'Dogs are really good at sniffing out spirit activity,' said Troy eagerly. 'My dog is, anyway – she's called Pepper, she's a terrier – but we had to leave her behind to come here.'

Tinkerbell clung tightly to Wuffly, as if imagining they might be wrenched apart at any second. 'Do you miss her?'

Troy nodded.

'Ryan?' said Max.

Ryan shrugged one shoulder as if he wasn't bothered – but his neck was going red again, and Pea guessed he was remembering the money in the tea rooms.

'Yeah, I reckon they've been pretty handy so far,' he said quietly.

'All right with you two?' asked Mum.

Pea looked at Tinkerbell. It *would* be fun, having some other people to mess around with. The boys knew what ectoplasm was. And though Ryan wasn't at all like Sam One, she thought he might be just as interesting to be friends with.

'We are *very* busy being the Thrilling Three,' said Tinkerbell. 'But I suppose if it didn't interrupt all our important campfires, and picnics, and villain-hunting—'

'You get to have campfires? Really?' said Troy.

'Well, we haven't had one yet – but we will. And we've got a tent. And a dog, obviously.'

Troy made a small whimpery noise of longing.

'We'd still be the Thrilling Three, though.'

'We could be the Thrilling Five,' suggested Pea.

'But what about PIE?' said Troy doubtfully. 'I don't want to not be PIE.'

'Thrilling PIE?' said Pea. 'So it's half us, and half you.'

'That sounds nuts,' said Ryan. Then he smiled. 'I like it.'

'We'll need a new logo,' said Tinkerbell.

'And a new handshake,' said Troy.

'And we'll need your balloon there,' said Ryan,

'so we can post a new video on our website about the castle ghost.'

'Can we help? Make the video, I mean?' asked Pea.

Mum and Max had a little chat, and it was all arranged. Pea and Tinkerbell would come over the very next morning to do just that.

'Why *should* you never play hide-and-seek with a ghost's mum and dad?' asked Tinkerbell on the doorstep, when they were on their way out.

Troy grinned as he knelt to ruffle Wuffly's ears. 'Because they're *trans-parents*!'

'That's awful,' said Tinkerbell, but she giggled as she said it.

Ryan had ducked out of sight, but he reappeared at the last minute. 'Hey, Pea? You said you wanted to borrow this, right?' he said in a low voice. He pressed *100 Paranormal Mysteries Explained!* into her hands.

Pea frowned at the image of the Loch Ness Monster on the cover. 'Um – I don't—'

'You should look at page sixteen especially,' Ryan said, and he lowered his sunglasses enough to shoot her a meaningful look over the top.

'Oh! Yes. Thanks.'

On the way home, she sneaked a peek inside. Tucked in between pages sixteen and seventeen was the money Ryan had borrowed.

Mum raised an enquiring eyebrow, but Pea tried to make her face expressionless as she slid the money into her pocket, and kept her smile to herself. It felt wonderfully Blyton-ish to be passing secret messages.

'Best Thing, Worst Thing?' Pea asked Tinkerbell that night as she was climbing into her top bunk.

'Best Thing: we've got friends with iPads. Two iPads. One each! I didn't even know that was a thing that could happen until we met them. Worst Thing, um . . . we've got less than a week left before we go back to boring London.'

Pea curled up in her bunk, thought of her To-Do List, and smiled. She would fetch herself a sticker tomorrow.

# CHAPTER 14

# THRILLING PIE

The next morning there were two envelopes on the mat again: one from Clem, one from Clover.

To: Kids
Doing loads better out of hospital
in a few days then home to rest
best love big hugs and kisses love
Dad/Clem STOP

'I don't think Clem ever did telegrams at school,' said Mum, with a smile. 'But didn't he do well for a first try?'

There were two more ten-pound notes in the envelope too.

'*Fudge*,' whispered Tinkerbell, gazing at the money. This time Pea didn't bother to argue.

The other was edged with blue forget-me-nots, and addressed in Clover's familiar curly handwriting.

Dear everyone,

Wondrous news! I have been given a starring role in Peter Pan!

The auditions were not like the ones at drama club. Here they make you audition in front of everyone, so if you forget your lines or your song comes out a bit wobbly, they all know, and whisper about you in an unkind way. Then the teachers pin up a list outside the auditorium so that everyone else finds out if you've got a proper part or if you are only playing scenery or Fourth Pirate (Non-Speaking).

Not that I have anything like that to worry about, obviously!

I will now have a lot of extra rehearsals - Dangling classes for the flying scenes, etc., so please don't worry if I forget to phone. Unfortunately the big performance is only for agents, talent-spotters, etc., so you definitely can't come. DON'T PHONE THEM UP TO ASK FOR TICKETS OR ANYTHING LIKE THAT. Anyway, I expect once I've learned how to Dangle, I will be doing it regularly on the London stage.

Please write to me with all your news. Of course I am having the most perfect and wondrous time but occasionally I have a spare five minutes to miss you in.

Kisses,
Clover x

Pea read the letter aloud, while Mum tapped away at the laptop.

'What's that? She got the part she wanted?' Mum said vaguely, not looking up. 'How lovely. Do you know, I wasn't at all sure that Cheseman Hall place would suit her, but Clover always lands on her feet, doesn't she?'

Pea read the letter again, frowning. There was something odd about it she couldn't quite put her finger on. What was 'a starring role'? Was she Peter Pan, or someone else?

There was no time to wonder, though. Mum clamped her headphones on (*Ocean Sounds Volume II* again). Tinkerbell put on her bobble-hat and her newly-created badge: an orange circle with *Thrilling* PIE written on it in green. Wuffly's lead was clipped on, and they marched off to Castle Cottage, with promises not to bother Mum all day long – unless Tinkerbell broke anything expensive-looking, or human.

'Welcome, fellow investigators!' boomed Max

as he opened the tomato-red front door. 'And dog. Go on upstairs, girls – PIE HQ is in the back bedroom.'

Pea, Tinkerbell and Wuffly hurried up, turned right on the landing, then stopped dead with a gasp. Ryan and Troy were dressed in their usual hoodies, and surrounded by equipment – not in a jumble like the messy room downstairs, but all laid out neatly: two laptops, one of the iPads, walkie-talkies, various strange objects with dials and aerials, a video camera, and a telescope on a stand at a very large window – looking directly out at the castle.

Not from a distance, like the view from the common. The castle was practically *in* the garden – one vast tower and a line of tumbledown wall looming up over the back hedge.

'Not bad, eh?' said Ryan, with a grin. 'There's a better view from the tea rooms garden, but they don't let you sleep there.'

'Dad did ask,' said Troy as Wuffly bounced over to give him a friendly bark hello.

**187**

'Always worth a try,' said Max, puffing up the stairs to join them.

Whenever they had friends over, Mum always left them to it – but to Pea's surprise, Max sat down in a cosy armchair, yawned, then began tapping away on a laptop. It looked very tiny under his big hands.

'So – schedule for the day: shoot a new video, upload to website, further Grey Lady research to get the new recruits up to speed, maybe a tour out in the car this afternoon to get some extra footage, if Ryan needs a bit of a rest – what do you say?'

'Is ghost-hunting, like, your actual proper job, then?' asked Tinkerbell, clearly just as confused as Pea.

Max laughed. 'I wish! No – I'm in computers – programming, that sort of thing – but I mostly work on that in the night, after the boys are asleep. These two live with their mother. I only get them four times a year, so I like to pack plenty in.

Working on PIE, it's sort of the thing we do together – right, lads?'

It was the holiday they were supposed to have had with Clem, Pea thought. All fun, to squash a whole year's worth of Dad time into a space too small for it.

Ryan fussed around at the desk, setting up the laptop and clicking the video camera screen out, ready to record.

While his left hand was busy, his right arm drifted upwards, bending towards him as if it was floating in water.

'Hand down, Ryan,' murmured Max, still typing.

Ryan sighed crossly, and his arm dropped back down sharply.

'Hey! Why did it do that?' said Tinkerbell.

'Tink!' Pea felt her cheeks glow, although she longed to know the answer. Then she realized she was staring too. 'Sorry.'

Ryan shrugged. 'Sometimes I kind of forget

that side of me's there, so it does stuff without me and I have to concentrate and tell it not to. It's a hemi thing.'

'Ryan has hemiplegia,' said Max. 'Something happened in his brain before he was born; an injury – a bit like a stroke, if you know what that is. It's just a fancy way of saying one side of him doesn't work quite as well as it should – right, Ry?'

'Does it mean half your brain doesn't work too?' asked Tinkerbell.

'Tink!'

'Mum said we should ask questions if we had questions!'

'Only if Ryan doesn't mind, she said.' Pea blushed; now Ryan knew they'd talked about him. 'Do you mind if we ask you things?'

Ryan gnawed his lip. 'Depends what they are.'

They asked about his 'hemi hand' (yes, the lycra splint got sweaty but felt quite nice, like a hug to wake up his sleepy arm; no, he didn't have to wear it in bed), and his leg (which sometimes had a splint on too, a hard one over his sock, though he'd had some operations and injections to stop him walking on tiptoe and didn't always have to wear it now), and what was horriblest about having hemiplegia (boring physio, strangers saying mean things, being stared at, and always being picked last in PE even when he was *definitely* the best at shooting basketball hoops). And there was something wrong with his brain, actually, so it had re-wired itself like the insides of a computer to find new ways to do things – which meant some-times the wires got crossed over, and the messages got scrambled.

'Like with your arm?' said Pea, feeling very guilty indeed about the staring.

Ryan nodded.

Pea wiggled her fingers, and tried to imagine what it would feel like if she couldn't tell them to pick up a pencil, or hold a book while the other hand turned the page.

'There's a thing or two you can't see, too,' added

Max. 'Maths isn't his favourite, is it, Ry? Because it's hard for him to keep written-down numbers in the right order. Since that re-wired brain is working extra-hard, it gets tired quicker, so sometimes he gets a bit . . . stroppy.' Ryan made a growly noise, but Max grinned unapologetically as he continued. 'Oh, and he likes pineapple on pizza. Oddest thing about him by far.'

'OK,' said Tinkerbell. 'I'm bored. Can we make the video now?'

'*Please*,' said Ryan feelingly.

And that was that.

Tinkerbell appointed herself director, as that involved the most shouting, and meant she got to hold the camera. She made Max do lighting, since he was tall enough to hold a lamp overhead without difficulty. Pea was script editor, writing out a speech on cards in extra-big letters (they all helped with the words). Troy was the card holder, standing next to Tinkerbell and dropping the cards in turn. Ryan did the presenting.

It took four tries to get it all finished. The first time Tinkerbell forgot to press the RECORD button. The second version was all jumbly because Troy got the cards mixed up. In the third, Tinkerbell shouted 'Action Man!' instead of 'Action!' and Ryan started laughing and couldn't stop. In the fourth version, Wuffly ran into shot when Ryan held up the balloon, and tried to bite it – but Pea said it added 'home-made charm', and with a nod from Max, everyone agreed.

Max hooked up the camera to the laptop. Ryan showed Pea how to add extra clips into the video, and titles on the beginning. They added credits at the end too, like on a TV show. It was quite thrilling, seeing AGENT PEA LLEWELLYN scroll up in green at the end. Then they put it on the website, so other people could find it – with a little article below by Pea. She included lots of Blyton facts, in case people who were more interested in her than in ghosts saw it.

'I reckon that's our best ever video,' said Max, sitting back proudly.

Troy nodded. 'Even better than the one about the Phantom Squid of Musselburgh, and that one has an actual squid in it.'

'A ghost squid, you mean,' said Tinkerbell.

'No, it really *was* just a squid in the end,' said Ryan, with a mournful sigh.

After a while Max fell asleep. The fuzzy hairs of his beard vibrated every time he snored.

'Don't worry – he does that a lot,' explained Troy, putting a blanket over his big tummy.

While Max snoozed, they spent the rest of the morning on octopus jokes ('What do you call an octopus that tells the time? A clocktopus!'), staring at the castle through the telescope, and looking through the Munros' collection of ghost-hunting books. Apparently, to find the Grey Lady, they should look out for floating spheres of light, and a clammy chill in the air – as if you'd just opened the fridge.

'That's how Dad knows his first encounter was genuine,' said Ryan softly. 'It happened in our old house: a figure of a girl, all dressed in rags, standing in a shaft of sunlight at the top of the stairs. Mum still says it was a trick of the light, a reflection of a painting on the wall, or something – but the chill in the air she brought with her, on a warm summer day . . . Dad reckons he'll never forget it.'

Pea shivered. It was scary, but thrilling, to believe.

'Did you see it too?' she whispered – but Ryan and Troy both shook their heads.

'That's why we *really* want to see the Grey Lady,' said Troy.

Pea's stomach rumbled, and she sneaked a peek at her watch. It was well past their usual lunch time.

'I'm hungry,' said Tinkerbell. 'When's lunch?'

'Don't be cheeky,' hissed Pea, secretly rather relieved.

But the boys didn't seem to think it was cheeky. They didn't seem to think 'lunch time' was a thing that happened at all: apparently they just helped themselves to food when they felt like it, or asked Max to cook something. It didn't even need to be all at the same time, or eating the same food.

They left Max snoring, and hurried downstairs.

Tinkerbell piled chunks of watermelon onto a plate next to seven slices of cheese and a big piece of home-made chicken pie from the fridge. Ryan fetched a packet of crisps (opening it with his teeth), ate a handful, then left the rest of the packet on the side. Troy made them both sandwiches with about half a jar of peanut butter. Neither of them had washed their hands first. This couldn't possibly be allowed.

But Pea squashed down all such Anne-ish thoughts, and had half a sandwich (apricot jam), a slice of warmed-up pizza, green olives (which she didn't like, it turned out), and a chocolate biscuit, all piled on the same plate. She even ate the chocolate biscuit first.

'This,' said Tinkerbell, after the sixth slice of cheese, 'is the best lunch ever. I can't wait to tell Mum she's doing it wrong.'

# CHAPTER
# 15

# GOOD NEWS

### Saturday 1 August

Dear Diary,
Today was brilliant! After we'd made videos
we went to the outdoor gym and the horse-
faced swing thing. We had races on the leg-
swinging machine and Ryan beat me *and* Tink. I
think he was showing off a bit but I suppose
that is allowed when you have one arm that
sometimes floats off without you. Then we

showed Den #2 to Ryan and Troy. They were a bit sad it didn't have a campfire, but I think they were impressed by the secret pocket that has chocolate digestives in. Then they had to go home so Ryan could have a rest. (Apparently that is a thing he has to do sometimes, because he really does get stroppy – even more than Tink that time Clem let her eat a whole bag of Haribo.)

Mum shouted at us for not telling Max where we were going even though he was asleep, but I think that was mostly because we distracted her in the middle of a good bit with piratical cannons in. (I do feel a bit guilty, though. I blame the Blyton fumes.)

We have lent Ryan and Troy some Enid Blytons so they know how to be Thrilling Three-ish, and the first *Mermaid Girls* book because it's about mermaids. I am still reading *100 Paranormal Mysteries Explained!* It is a bit disappointing about the Loch Ness Monster.

I still don't know what part Clover has in *Peter Pan*. I tried phoning her to tell her about Thrilling PIE, but I suppose you have to switch off your phone if you are learning to Dangle.

Tink really really wants to see the Grey Lady, even more than smugglers, kidnappings, etc. But I'm a bit scared, so it's OK if it doesn't happen.

---

### Sunday 2 August

Dear Diary,

Today was brilliant again!

Clem phoned to say he is not in hospital any more and is feeling lots better - hooray! We have sent him a card with a drawing of the Grey Lady on it. Tinkerbell wanted to wait until we'd actually seen her, but I said an artistic impression will do till then. Apparently the Grey Lady has three guns and an axe.

In the morning we went to the beach to look for mermaids. Max watched the sea with binoculars. We mainly made a sandcastle. Troy said the *Mermaid Girls* is a girl book so he isn't allowed it. Tinkerbell hit him on the head with a sand bucket. (I found him reading it later anyway.)

In the afternoon Max took us shopping in his car and bought a tent. He says it isn't for camping in, it's for taking with them if PIE need to sit on a hill to look out for ghosts (apparently ghosts don't mind rain). I said we could have lent them ours – but theirs is a posh one that pops up by itself and has no pointy ends of poles. I wonder if this is 'glamping', like what Sam One is doing.

Ryan has lent me *Haunted Scotland: A Catalogue*. Scotland really is very haunted.

No wonder all the Scottish people I know are ghost-hunters.

Mum's written three more chapters! Coraly the ghost mermaid has still not turned up, but Mum says that's because all those inky tormentulas got in the way. I have left *Haunted Scotland: A Catalogue* next to her in case she needs reminding.

I've started a new story called *Spookadoo Hall.* It is about a haunted house and a girl called Marie who moves there and finds out it is a haunted house. I don't know what happens after that because I have been quite busy.

Clover still isn't answering her phone.

Tinkerbell said that if Thrilling PIE don't see the Grey Lady before we have to go home on Friday, she will cry. Maybe I should've put the Grey Lady on my To-Do List.

'Perhaps we need some sort of magic spell to make her appear,' sighed Tinkerbell, when Pea finished reading her bedtime *Famous Five*.

But there was no need. The next morning Pea and Tinkerbell were eating Weetabix in their pyjamas when there was a frantic hammering at the front door.

On the doorstep was Troy, so sweaty and breathless his glasses were steamed up – with Ryan following behind.

'We've got her!' he panted. 'The Grey Lady! We've got her on video!'

'It's true,' puffed Ryan, catching up. 'Got picked up by the security camera in the sweet shop last night, about two in the morning. They saw our flyer and showed it to us. Dad's at home putting it on the website. We can show you now,' he added producing an iPad.

Pea and Tinkerbell flung coats and wellies on over their pyjamas, and they dashed as quietly as possible out to Den #2. (Mum was already typing away, and there was an ominous note pinned to the living-room door.)

Interruptions Only
from people with
biscuits or bleeding
head wounds

Pea and Tinkerbell stared open-mouthed at the video on the iPad. First it was just a boring black-and-white view of the village in the dark. But slowly a strange mist began to fill the square, like a low-lying fog – and a figure, all in white, glided into view. It was a woman with her hair tied up in a bun under a cloth cap, and a full-length dress. She carried an old-fashioned lantern with a glowing candle inside. And every inch of her was white: her skin, her clothes, even her hair under its cap – everything but her eyes, which were a pure, terrifying coal-black.

She moved slowly, gliding as if her feet weren't touching the ground, her head turning slowly from side to side, searching for something.

Then she drifted towards the castle mound, out of view of the camera. Gradually the mist faded away, and the village square went back to looking quite ordinary.

Pea shivered.

'That's brilliant,' whispered Tinkerbell.

They watched it again, and again. It seemed eerier each time.

'She's not grey, though,' said Pea eventually. 'And she's got a head.'

'So?' said Ryan.

'I wasn't complaining! It's just not what I expected.'

If she was honest, Pea realized she hadn't really expected to see a ghost at all – but Ryan and Troy were so thrilled, it was impossible not to feel thrilled too.

Once Pea and Tinkerbell were dressed, they all hurried off to Castle Cottage.

'Isn't it incredible?' said Max, his beard quivering with the excitement. 'We've got her – we've actually got her!'

They spent the morning dashing around the village, handing out PIE flyers and asking if anyone had spotted any mysterious balls of light, or blobs of ectoplasm. After another help-yourself lunch, Max collected their new tent, his deck-chair, and a backpack with all his special tracking equipment. Ryan and Troy filled up their utility belts with EMF detectors and walkie-talkies, and Troy clipped first Ryan's, then his, round their waists.

'What can we bring?' whispered Tinkerbell, looking nervous. (She'd given up the sticky-tape belt; it kept sticking her to other things, like sofas, and Wuffly.)

'We'll just bring ourselves and our clever brains,

like we did with the Enid Blyton ghost,' Pea said confidently. 'I'll bring pencil and paper as well, just in case. And you bring Wuffly – dogs are good at tracking spirits, remember?'

First they headed for the castle gates – since, as Pea said, that was where it looked like the Grey Lady had been going. Tinkerbell scanned Eliza the archer, much to her amusement – but the EMF detector only hummed, instead of buzzing and squealing.

Then they went over the bridge and halfway up the very steep hill that looked over the castle mound, stopping just level with the lower walls. Ryan fell over a few times on the way up, but he just stuck out an arm, without having to say a word, and Troy helped him up. Pea made sure she walked slowly, so he wouldn't feel left behind.

Max popped the tent up awkwardly, at an angle. He lay down in it so it wouldn't blow away – and fell asleep again.

'Just when it's getting exciting too,' said Troy,

shaking his head in disgust.

They made a miniature camp halfway up the hill, spreading out all their kit. Wuffly kept sniffing out exciting trails and sending Troy and Tinkerbell leaping gleefully after her into the brambles – though it was always a rabbit, never a ghost. Pea and Ryan sat in the grass, taking turns with the binoculars to monitor the castle, the video camera close by in case the Grey Lady reappeared. Every now and then a tourist or a hiker would wander past, and they would politely ask if anyone had seen a ghost – headless or otherwise – floating about.

No one had, but almost all of them smiled and promised to keep an eye out.

Ryan scanned the horizon with the binoculars, then trained them on the castle again. He watched calmly for a while, then threw them aside in frustration.

'Argh! Sorry. It's just – she's so close, you know? It's almost worse, knowing she's out there for real, and we still might not get a glimpse of her.'

Pea nodded. She wanted it too: to feel that eerie chill and know she had seen the real thing with her own eyes.

'It's for . . .' Ryan checked anxiously over his shoulder – but Max was still asleep, and Troy and Tinkerbell were off in the brambles. 'It's for my dad more than anything,' he added, in a low voice. 'Our mum's nice – bit of a fusser, always nagging on at me to put my heel down, put my hand down, *keep a lid on your temper Ryan* – but she's not a believer. She thinks Dad's nuts, *wasting all his money on toys to play ghosties with, like a big kid.*' He fiddled with his twirly shoelaces. 'And like he said, he only gets us four times a year. So it's got to all be good, right? It's got to be perfect.'

Pea thought of help-yourself lunches, and the brand-new pop-up tent, and the flashy website they'd all made together. It was amazing – but somehow frightening at the same time: like Christmas every day, with none of the exciting part where you got to look forward to it.

'Is that why they split up, your mum and dad – because Max believes in ghosts, and she doesn't?'

Ryan half shrugged. 'No. Well . . . yes. I don't know. I think it was a bunch of things.'

'Mum and my dad weren't ever really together,' said Pea, with a frown. 'And with Clem – that's Tink's dad, though me and Clover, that's my other sister, we sort of use him as ours too – I'm not really sure.' She picked up the binoculars, wiping grass off the lenses. 'Do you ever feel like it was your fault?'

'No!'

'I didn't mean that you should! Only, people do. Sometimes.'

In books, she meant, or on television. And when Clem had left, a little bit.

The smell of fizzy orange pop drifted into Pea's nose. She'd spilled some on Clem's work shirts, just before he left. He'd ironed them into a perfect pile and left them in the basket on a kitchen chair ready for the morning. She'd taken the fizzy orange out of the fridge, and the bottle had slipped out of her hand, bouncing on the floor and getting all shaken up so that when she opened it, a fountain of fizz sprayed out – all over Pea, and all over the shirts. It was an accident. She hadn't meant it; if she could've rewound time for even a second, she would. But he was angry, and he'd shouted at her, and then Mum had shouted at both of them . . . and a week later Clem was sleeping on a friend's sofa and looking for a new flat to live in without them.

Although there was a large, sensible and quite correct part of Pea's brain which said that Clem didn't leave because of a bottle of fizzy orange – or because of her at all – there was still a tiny corner of her that believed it, mostly late at night, in the dark, when she couldn't sleep.

'Suppose I do a little bit,' muttered Ryan, squinting through the binoculars, his neck going red again. 'Reckon every kid does, right?'

Pea nodded.

She felt sad, suddenly, for all the Ryans and Troys and Tinkerbells and all the rest. It was a shame no one in Enid Blyton's stories ever had a fizzy orange memory of their own to worry about. But then she thought that maybe that was what she liked about some books most of all. They were a little world of safety, where nothing too awful could ever happen.

They sat quietly, watching tiny tourists walk around inside the castle.

Pea lifted the binoculars and scanned the ruins. She watched the steam train go by, the chuff of its engine echoing off the hills. Then she focused on the village. She could follow the same person from one street to the next from here: a young family – a girl and boy running to press their noses to the window of the bakery; an older couple walking slowly; a teenage girl with tumbly blonde hair under a top hat, dragging a fat blue suitcase with parcel tape holding it together.

Pea froze.

The girl in the top hat kept her head low as she hauled the battered suitcase past the bakery. Pea lost her for a moment, jerking the binoculars round too quickly as she tried to adjust the focus – but an instant later she found her again, right in the middle of the village square, looking up at the Enid Blyton shop and giving Pea a clear view of the side of her face.

Clover.

# A SURPRISING ARRIVAL

'We have to go,' Pea said, flinging down the binoculars. 'I'll explain later!'

'What? Where are we going?' yelled Tinkerbell, tugging Wuffly along behind her as Pea dragged her down the steep steps, away from the boys and over the bridge as quickly as she could. 'Why are we in such a— Oh!'

Clover shrieked the moment she saw them. She threw down the fat blue suitcase and flung her arms around them both.

'Oh, it's so lovely to see you! And hug you!

I've been hugging my photo but it's not at all the same!'

Pea hugged her back as tightly as she could, while Wuffly danced around her ankles.

'Hang on . . .' said Pea in a muffled voice. 'How are you here?'

Clover let go at last and took a step back, her eyes bright. 'I wanted to come and see you! I couldn't bear to think of you all having so much fun without me. So I hopped on a train.'

'But what about all your Cheese Camp lessons?' said Tinkerbell. 'And all your rehearsals for Peter Pan?'

Clover's eyes went shiny. 'Never mind all that – let's talk about you!'

They sat down on a bench. Tinkerbell explained all about Thrilling PIE, and catching the Grey Lady. Clover nodded eagerly, smiling as she tucked her arm into Pea's. But Pea noticed that she kept looking over her shoulder, and every now and then her breath would come out in a jerky little

gasp. Her usually round pink cheeks looked pale –
and the blue suitcase seemed every bit as stuffed as
when she'd left London, as if she'd packed *all* her
things to come and visit.

'Clover,' said Pea eventually, 'do the theatre
camp people know you're here?'

'Mmm,' said Clover, nodding, but without
meeting Pea's eye.

Tinkerbell gasped. 'Have you run away? Ooh.
That's brilliant. No, wait. You're going to be Peter
Pan and do flying. Why would you run away?'

There was an awful silence.

'I'm not Peter Pan,' Clover whispered. 'There
aren't any Dangling lessons. It's all dreadful
and . . . and everyone hates me!'

She held up her chin and pressed her lips
together, but they began to wobble, and the shini-
ness in her eyes overflowed into real tears.

Pea and Tinkerbell exchanged panicked looks.
Clover couldn't possibly have a weepathon in the
middle of the village square – especially not if

**216**

she'd run away and was supposed to be hiding. A sobbing fourteen-year-old in a top hat was bound to be noticed.

'Scones,' said Pea firmly. 'Scones and tea. They mend everything.'

They steered a sniffling Clover to a shady corner of the tea rooms garden, and Pea ordered a pot of tea and one big scone. Tinkerbell fed it into Clover in chunks, until she became less hiccupy.

'Thank you,' she croaked, clutching her cup of tea tightly. 'Thank you.'

'But what happened?' asked Pea. 'In your letters you sounded so happy.'

Clover shook her head. 'All fibs. I didn't want you to worry, Pea – not when you had Mum and Tink and Clem to worry about already.'

Tinkerbell folded her arms crossly. 'I'm not a worry.'

Clover patted Tinkerbell gently on the elbow. 'Of course not. I just meant Pea was a bit busy, that's all, and you were having so much fun I didn't want to spoil it. So I thought of all the things I wished were happening instead of all the horrible things that actually were – and pretended they were true, on the phone, and in my letters.'

'You made it all up? Even the Chin Acting?' Tinkerbell's eyes went wide.

Clover shuddered. 'Not that. That was real. And having to pretend to be a fruit bowl. But there wasn't any roast chicken. The food was horrid – those whippy mashed potatoes from a box. And soup – the thin sort, like salty water. All the Pawns had to share one huge freezing bathroom. Showers all in a row with no door on! Scratchy towels too. And lumpy beds.'

'Yuck,' said Tinkerbell.

Pea thought it sounded like an orphanage in a book: thrillingly tragic, but probably not much fun if you were living in it.

'It was very good acting,' she said. 'Honestly. We'd never have guessed.'

Clover managed a watery smile, before

dissolving into tears again. 'I'm glad you think so. No one at theatre camp thought I was any good at all! They've all been going there for years and years, and they all go to stage schools in term time, where they do jazz and tap and singing lessons every day. I had to go in all the beginners' classes, with the eight-year-olds, and even then I was the worst one.' She hung her head.

'So you aren't Peter Pan?'

'No. Agata is. I didn't make *her* up.' There was a sigh in Clover's voice as she said it. 'She's so pretty and talented and she's been in so many shows already, and I *so* wanted to be her friend. But when they found out I didn't already know every-thing, I got moved down to the Pawns, and she wouldn't talk to me any more. Usually the Pawns – that's the juniors – do a special dance to intro-duce the main show, but yesterday they decided I couldn't even be in that because I'm so much bigger than everyone else. At lunch they started calling me Clover the Hulk, and wobbled about when I walked by as if the ground was shaking.'

It was the sort of thing Pea could imagine happening to herself, but not Clover; never Clover. Her big sister twirled into every new room with a smile, and her happiness seemed to sweep people along with it like a tide, and make them smile too. She was the certainest person Pea knew, even more than Mum. And now she was sitting on a garden chair looking squashed, too sad to even swat the wasps off her last bit of scone. It was truly awful.

'Won't they come looking for you, if you've run away?' asked Pea.

Clover shook her head. 'Not likely. I pretended to be Mum, and phoned their office. *Hello, this is Bree Llewellyn. I'm so sorry, but there's been a family emergency, and my daughter Clover absolutely must come home to be with her sisters. Thank you, that's ever so kind – I'll call the moment the situation changes.*'

The imitation was so perfect it was as if Mum was right there, eating a scone.

Tinkerbell's jaw dropped open. 'Whoa. When

we get home, can you phone my teacher and do that next time I haven't done my homework?'

Clover beamed, a little of the pinkness returning to her cheeks.

'But . . . where are you going to stay?' said Pea.

Tinkerbell snorted. 'With us, of course! You can have my bunk bed. I'll sleep in the tent. I don't mind.'

Pea shook her head. 'We can't do that without Mum knowing. And . . . it's lovely you're here, and I'm so happy you aren't still somewhere that made you sad and called you a Hulk, but . . . we've only got five days of Blyton fumes left for Mum's book. She's in the proper scary writing zone, Clover.'

Clover looked alarmed. 'No showers, chin covered in biscuit crumbs?'

'She's on three custard creams before breakfast. And her desk's got The Smell.'

The Smell was a particular pong that wafted out of Mum's study when she was truly captivated by her work: a mixture of mouldering peppermint tea bags, cushions that have been sat on by many bottoms, and old toast.

Tinkerbell looked faintly sick – but they all knew it was a good sign.

'You can't interrupt The Smell. If you suddenly turn up on the doorstep, she'll feel awful about how miserable you've been. Or . . . she could even send you back.'

'She wouldn't!' said Tinkerbell.

'She might,' said Pea. 'Theatre camp cost lots of money. Granny Duff's money, but still, she wouldn't like it being wasted. Either way, she'd get all distracted again. It would be like when she was being a hamster and watching beige-wall television all day at home. She might never finish the book at all!'

Pea had worked so hard with the motivational stickers, and the having to be the boring sensible Anne one. She couldn't bear the thought of the *Pirate Girls* book lying half done, never to have an ending. But Clover was clutching the blue suitcase, a look of terror in her eyes. Pea couldn't send her away, either.

Tinkerbell, however, had a familiar wicked twinkle in her eye.

'I know *exactly* what to do,' she said.

That night, Pea and Tinkerbell put on their pyjamas extra early. Then they flopped on the sofa, and did meaningful yawning.

'Sorry, my starlings, I absolutely must get this pirate ship to sink before I stop for the night,' said Mum, tapping away without looking up. 'Go on up to bed.'

'But look, Mum, it's loads past your bedtime too,' said Tinkerbell in a sleepy voice.

Mum glanced at the clock, and gasped. Then she shook her head, grinning. 'Ha! That clock must be broken, Stinks. The one on the laptop says I've got another few hours.'

The clock was not broken – Tinkerbell had

sneaked in earlier, and wound the hands forward – but she hadn't thought of the one on the computer.

'Besides, you're on holiday. Doesn't matter if we're all a bit late to bed, hmm?'

In fact, it mattered rather a lot. Clover was hiding in Den #2 with the blue suitcase, waiting for an owl-noise to tell her it was safe to slip indoors to brush her teeth. There was a small bundle of extra-warm blankets and a torch ready for her in the kitchen, to take back out to the tent. But there were windows that looked out onto the garden, right beside the scrubbed pine table where Mum worked. Until Mum went up to bed, no one dared risk it.

Pea made cups of cocoa, and turned off all the lights except the one glowing lamp near Mum's table.

Tinkerbell made hinty snoring noises.

Wuffly genuinely fell asleep on Pea's lap.

In the end, they had to admit defeat. Wuffly

was carried to her cosy bed in the hall, and they trooped up to bed with Mum still working in the glow of the lamp.

'Shall we try to stay awake, so we can let her in?' whispered Tinkerbell.

Pea shook her head. 'Remember the night Mum had all that coffee? She could be up for hours. I don't think your plan is going to work, Tink. We can't do this every night till we go home! Mum's bound to look in the garden sooner or later.'

Tinkerbell stuck out her tongue. 'Pfft. If the real Famous Five had a person to hide, George would totally do risky brave things to help them. You're just not thinking George-ishly enough.'

She skipped down the stairs. 'Left my book in the tent – just going to fetch it!' she called.

'Mmm,' said Mum vaguely.

Pea heard the back door click. There was a lot of shuffling about and whispering. She waited at the top of the stairs, her heart in her mouth, expecting disaster at any moment – but a few minutes later, Tinkerbell tiptoed back up, grinning from ear to ear.

'See? Easy.'

She looked so proud and happy that Pea couldn't help grinning back.

Her To-Do List was going brilliantly.

The Grey Lady was real.

Clem was better.

Clover was home.

All was well.

# CHAPTER 17

# ALL IS NOT WELL

Pea's feeling of contentment did not last long.

Clover, it turned out, was not a natural camper.

The tent was too cold. The cushions were too lumpy. At some point in the night, a cow had walked past the gate at the end of the garden, and made such a noise that she hadn't got a wink of sleep. And the bathroom arrangements were not at all satisfactory.

'I had to wee behind a bush,' she wailed. 'In the rain! In the dark!'

'Oi! No moaning – you're getting breakfast in bed,' said Tinkerbell.

They had taken a tray up to Mum first, with one of Pea's pirate books so she'd stay there, out of the way. Then they'd piled boiled eggs and toasty soldiers onto plates, and carried them out under an umbrella. (It was raining again.)

It had done nothing to cheer Clover up. Neither did her reflection, when examined in the blade of a butter knife.

'Look at my hair! You have to let me inside to wash it. You need to wash all these clothes too. And bring me more blankets. And some crisps, in case I get hungry.'

Tinkerbell shook her head. 'No crisps. Crisps are noisy.'

'Popcorn, then. Or jelly babies. Actually, let me come to the shop, so I can choose.'

'You can't!' Pea squeaked. 'You have to stay here, in the tent. If you go out into the village, people will see you and they might tell Mum. She might see you sneaking in and out of the garden too. You can't be seen, Clover – it'll ruin the whole plan!'

'I can't stay in here for ever! I'll freeze! And die of boredom! A cow will come in and trample me to death! Can't I come ghost-hunting with you? I want to be in Thrilling PIE too.'

But Tinkerbell was just as firm. 'You're like an escaped prisoner. You're only allowed out when we say so. And you have to be quiet like a tiny little mouse.'

'You can have a sticker if you stay quietly hidden all morning. And another one for the afternoon,' said Pea.

'Why would I want a sticker?'

'They've got lemons on? And smiley pandas?'

Clover moaned, and flopped back on her cushions. 'This is worse than being a Pawn. Well, nearly.'

They left her with a pile of books and some extra toast, and promised to bring her a packed lunch later. Mum was already back at work in her pyjamas, lost in her headphones, tapping away.

The Munro boys were very impressed by their secret plan, once Troy had got over the idea they had another sister. They explained it all in whispers, while Max was packing up their day's supplies.

'Why's she not happy?' whispered Troy. 'I'd love to be a secret person hiding in a den.'

'I know! Proper camping,' sighed Tinkerbell. 'I'd live on berries and mushrooms and probably learn wolf language, and I wouldn't have a bath for a whole week.'

Pea wasn't sure Clover would survive not having a bath for even a day – not graciously, anyway.

They set off for another day's Grey Lady hunting with Max, all around the outside of the castle, asking a new batch of tourists if they'd spotted any ectoplasm lying around.

It was still fun, but Pea couldn't concentrate; not while she was worrying about Clover. She let Max walk on ahead, and hung back.

'What are we going to do with her, Tink?

We'll never keep her hidden till Friday!'

'Could she stay in your back garden, instead?' said Tinkerbell, looking at Ryan – but he shook his head.

'Not secretly. My dad'd be bound to tell your mum.' He shrugged. 'I don't know – maybe she'll turn out to be better at hiding than you think?'

But when they went into the castle's white-painted ticket office to hand out more flyers, Pea felt a tap on her shoulder.

'Ooh, are these your friends?' said a bright voice.

Pea spun round – to find a very odd-looking boy standing there. He wore a black wool hat pulled down over his eyebrows, an oversized coat with a furry hood, a familiar-looking pair of green plastic sunglasses shaped like palm trees and, most surprising of all, a curvy moustache.

The boy smiled. A bit of the moustache peeled off. Then Wuffly jumped up at him, and the boy gave her a good fond ruffle and a kiss on the nose

– which made the moustache fall off completely.

'Clover!' hissed Pea.

'Hello!' she said, dropping the sunglasses down an inch so they could see her blue eyes. 'Do you like my disguise?'

'Er,' said Ryan. 'Not really.'

'Can't stay, must dash!' said Troy, picking the moustache up off the ground. 'You know,' he continued, seeing their puzzled faces, 'must dash – moustache?'

'Oh, that's good! Hello – you must be Ryan and Troy. I'm here to help find your ghostly woman thingy.'

'No, you're not!' yelped Pea. 'You're supposed to be hiding!'

'Oh, I got fed up. You can't really expect me to sit in a wet tent all day. I'm meant to be on holiday too, you know.'

'Hello, hello,' said Max. 'Who's your friend?'

'Hi, I'm . . . Billybob,' said Clover, her voice switching suddenly from her usual one to a low growl halfway through the sentence as she fumbled the moustache back onto her face. 'Um. A cousin. Just visiting.'

'Billybob? And Pea and Tinkerbell – you *are* a creative lot, I must say,' said Max, raising an eyebrow, then giving an approving nod. 'We're going off to the Visitor Centre next, I think, if your cousin wants to come with us? Or are you giving him the guided tour of the village first?'

Clover gave Pea a pleading look over the rain-speckled palm-tree sunglasses.

Pea hesitated. It was bad enough that Max had seen her, but the sooner he forgot about Billybob the better. They might as well go exploring.

'Guided tour. We'll, um, see you later?'

Wuffly danced around Clover's legs again, then began to drag Tinkerbell away, towards the path around the castle.

'Thank you!' said Clover, twirling.

'Just keep your hood up! And don't twirl! Look out for Mum too, just in case she decides to come out and breathe in some extra Blyton fumes.'

Wuffly led them down the hill. They went through the trees, across the stream and back up the steep, slippery hill with the steps in it, past where she'd spotted Clover yesterday, all the way to the windswept top where they'd hoped to put Den #1.

Just as they reached the flat, brambly top of the hill, the clouds parted, and bright shafts of sunlight beamed through the gaps, lighting up the castle ruins below.

'Ooh,' said Tinkerbell.

'It's freezing up here. But I suppose it *is* sort of beautiful,' said Clover, with a sigh.

Even though there was a smell of cowpats, and her knee was damp where she'd slipped on the way up, and doing her To-Do List had left her feeling really quite tired, Pea wished they could stay in Corfe Castle village for ever. Mum would write the best books here. They could hunt ghosts all day long. They could go to the beach to look for mermaids whenever they felt like it. There would always be scones and ice cream and not-ginger beer.

That was the sad thing about holidays: they always ended. It was hard not to let knowing that spoil the parts that were still left.

She tried taking a picture with the phone, of Clover and Tinkerbell's backs against the sunlit sky. But Wuffly wouldn't keep still, and it looked small and grey compared to the real thing. She shut her eyes instead, and tried to catch a few images in her memory, to tell Clem about later.

'Oh, look – a fire circle,' came Clover's voice, wafting from somewhere behind Pea. 'People must come up here at night and have campfires.'

'The castle has lights on it when it gets dark.' That was Tinkerbell, hopping about somewhere to Pea's right. 'I bet it looks brilliant from up here.'

'Ow!' yelped Clover. 'Who's left a big spike sticking up out of the grass?'

'Get down, Wuffly! Let me have a look. It's not a spike. It's a tent peg. Ooh, people must camp up here too.'

'My big toe wishes they wouldn't.'

'Look, there's an old fork as well. They must have cooked on their campfire. Sausages, probably.'

'You can't know that, Tink.'

'Well, that's what I'd have, if it was us.'

Wuffly barked her agreement.

Pea opened her eyes with a start. The sky was bright, and tears sprang into them at once – but she felt a big swell of excitement in her chest. She wiped her eyes and turned to her sisters.

'I've got an idea,' she said.


One phone call and twenty minutes later, Pea, Tinkerbell and 'Billybob' waited anxiously outside Castle Cottage, until the red front door swung open.

'It's OK – we sent Dad out to buy new batteries for the EMF detectors,' said Ryan, beckoning them in. 'He'll be ages. Now, what's this big new secret plan?'

They all gathered on the massive leather sofas. Pea was trembling so much with hopeful nerves she could barely speak.

'I think – I mean, I thought – I mean, maybe . . . we could go camping,' she said. 'Tonight. Proper camping – secretly, all of us, up on the top of the hill.'

'Whoa,' said Tinkerbell. 'That's the sort of bonkers plan *I'd* come up with.'

'I'd have to wee on a bush again,' said Clover, appalled. 'And it's raining.'

'By ourselves, you mean?' said Ryan. 'Without Dad?'

Pea's shoulders sagged. 'You're right. It's a terrible idea – we'd get into tons of trouble, I don't know why I even thought—'

'What? It's a *brilliant* idea!' yelled Tinkerbell, leaping up. 'Clover, you've already weed on a bush once, so doing it again won't matter. If you're not

**237**

hiding in the back garden, Mum's loads less likely to find you and send you back to horrible Cheese Man Camp – and we can't distract her if we aren't there. We'd be camping by a castle, *the* castle, like the real, actual Famous Five. And we can stay up all night, looking for the Grey Lady.'

Ryan sucked in a deep breath.

'With a campfire?' asked Troy.

'Of course! Please please please can we? Can we really? Say yes, Clover, please?'

'Why am I the one who has to say yes?'

'Because you're the oldest now,' said Tinkerbell. 'Sorry, Pea.'

Pea shook her head happily. 'I don't mind.'

She really didn't. She was fairly sure that it was, in fact, a terrible plan – but Clover was practically an adult. If she said it was all right to camp on a hill in secret, then it would be.

'I suppose it wouldn't be *that* different from camping in the back garden . . .' said Clover slowly.

'Hooray!' yelled Tinkerbell.

'But wait – what will you tell Mum? She doesn't know I'm here. I don't think she'd say yes to the two of you camping out here by yourselves.'

Ryan and Troy exchanged gloomy looks.

'Dad definitely wouldn't,' said Ryan.

Clover looked as if she might be changing her mind – but Tinkerbell grinned.

'Clover, you know how you phoned the Cheese Man people and pretended to be Mum? And you know how you've been doing accents at Cheese Camp? Have you done any Scottish ones?'

Clover nodded warily.

'I know *exactly* what to do.'

It took a little bit of practice, with tips from the boys – 'A wee bit deeper,' said Ryan, 'and roll your "r"s more' – and Clover was ready. She stuck on her peeled-off fake moustache and the top hat – 'to help me get into character' – and gave Pea a nod.

Pea picked up the mobile phone, took a deep breath, and called Mum.

'Um. Hi, Mum, it's Pea. No, nothing's wrong. Only, you know how you said that when we were out of the way, you got loads of work done? Max had an idea. Or, well, we sort of *all* did. Um . . . Can we go and stay with them tonight? We'd take the tent, and camp in their back garden. So you'd be all undistracted, and we could have lots of fun. Max says it's OK. He's here, if you want to ask him anything?'

Pea felt her mouth go dry as she handed over the phone, crossing her fingers that Mum would be too distracted by *Pirate Girls* to notice that the voice on the phone didn't quite sound like Max – but Clover slipped quite naturally into the role. Clover-Max promised to call if there were any problems, and to send Tinkerbell home at once if she crumpled, snapped or ate anything of value in Castle Cottage.

'So thoughtful of you, I'm so grateful – and I'm sure my girls are too,' said Mum.

'*My pleasurrrre*,' said Clover-Max, and hung up.

Then she whipped off her moustache, took a deep breath, and called Max in her best Mum-voice, to ask if the boys could come to stay in *their* garden. It took a bit more effort this time, and Clover had to promise it was only for one night, and to take walkie-talkies, and to help Ryan with changing into his pyjamas if he needed it (Ryan's neck went very red). But in the end he sounded quite happy.

Clover put down the phone, and looked around with anxious pale blue eyes. 'Was that all right?'

'Those Cheese people are idiots,' said Tinker-bell. 'You're the best actor in the whole world.'

# CHAPTER
# 18

# DEN #1

The rest was, to Pea's astonishment, remarkably easy.

'Thrilling PIE and Agent Billybob to rendez-vous at 1600 hours – that's four o'clock – on the bridge at the bottom of the hill. OK?' said Ryan, checking his watch against Pea's.

'OK,' she said, giggling; both their hands were shaking from the excitement.

They ran home across the common, Tinkerbell singing a made-up song as they went (the lyrics of which were: *Thrilling PIE, Thrilling PIE, Thrilling PIE, Thrilling PIE! Oooo-oooh! We are Thriüülling*

*PIE! We are going, to find, a ghost* – to the tune of *Doctor Who*). Pea found herself humming it as she collected clothes, camping supplies (like torches, and bottles of drinking water), and toothbrushes.

Tinkerbell took down the tent.

Clover was meant to hide outside the garden gate looking after their mounting pile of gear, but she refused to spend another night camping without a proper wash, and insisted on being smuggled into the house for a shower. She put the Billybob disguise back on, which Pea felt would probably not help if Mum happened to see her, but she supposed it was better than nothing.

Mum, meanwhile, sat typing furiously, headphones on, and did not notice a thing: not Pea carefully removing some of the mouldering tea-mugs, nor Tinkerbell sneaking a frying pan and a packet of sausages out of the kitchen, nor Billybob slipping down the stairs – now with long blonde curls and ponging of lavender body spray.

The pile of things was far too big to carry,

especially with Clover's suitcase. But Tinkerbell remembered the old sledge in the shed, with its metal runners.

'I know it's meant to go on snow,' she said. 'But we can still pull it over grass, can't we?'

They gave it a few test runs, with Wuffly sitting on it, and Pea and Tinkerbell pulling the rope at the front. It was hard work, but still easier than trying to carry everything by hand.

Clover hid behind the hedge while they went inside to say goodbye.

Pea had to unplug the headphones and waft a custard cream under Mum's nose before she even noticed them.

'Oh! You're off? Have a wonderful time, my chicks!' she said. 'Say thank you to Max, lots of times. Very, very best behaviour, Stinks – yes? And promise to come back tomorrow to check that I'm being a good girl too, won't you?'

There were hugs, then Pea and Tinkerbell headed out of the back door. They were at the gate, about to whoop with relief, when Mum suddenly appeared in the garden.

'Pea?' she called.

With a squeak, Clover ducked back out of sight.

Pea walked solemnly back down the path, certain they were discovered. It was a terrible plan, she knew it, she'd known it all along . . .

But Mum stroked her ponytail, and gave her a tired but very fond smile. 'I have a funny feeling this was all your idea,' she said. 'Thank you for being such a thoughtful big sister, and the best Neditor, and my favourite Pea in the whole wide world.'

Mum gave her a kiss, then pressed a little round sticker on Pea's jumper: a yellow sun with a happy face, and WELL DONE! written underneath.

They set off across the common, Pea glowing with pride all the way.

It was hard work, even with the sledge bumping along behind them. Clover's blue suitcase kept falling off, threatening to burst open again and send all her socks and moustaches flying. In the end Pea made her drag it along herself. But they made it to the rendezvous only a few minutes late.

Ryan and Troy were waiting in full PIE uniform, sunglasses on, with their tent and a backpack stuffed with kit.

'Agents Troy and Ryan, reporting for duty!' said Troy. Then he and Ryan did their complicated handshake.

'Only just,' said Ryan, looking very relieved. 'Dad wanted to drop us off in the car and say hi to your mum. We only got away without because he fell asleep.'

They set off to drag all their things up to the top of the hill. Pea saw Ryan hesitate at the bottom, wiping his forehead and looking up at the very steep, very slippery slope. They'd been halfway up it with Max, but never all the way to the top.

'All OK there, Agent Ryan?' said Pea.

'Let's find out, eh?' said Ryan, sliding his sunglasses on.

It turned out that he could manage quite well, if

slowly, with a bit of falling over and someone walking behind him with a hand at his shoulder to keep him steady. As he approached the top, he did some of it sitting down, taking long rests – and the very last section was done holding tightly to the sledge, laughing so hard he nearly fell off, while Clover and Pea pulled and Tinkerbell and Troy pushed.

At the top he lay flat out on the grass while the others went back down the hill to fetch the rest of their gear.

Then they mucked about, finding all the little dips and hollows, and testing out grass-sledging.

'I need ice cream,' panted Tinkerbell, flopping down beside the fire-circle.

'I need another shower,' said Clover.

'Tent first,' said Pea. 'Before it rains again and everything gets soggy.'

They found two uncowpatty spots. The Munros' tent popped up at once, so the boys helped Tinkerbell and Pea with theirs.

'We're like proper outdoors holiday people in

the countryside,' said Tinkerbell dreamily, lying down inside with her head poking out. 'Proper real campers.'

Clover reached into her suitcase for her body spray, and squirted her lavender pong all around them. 'Campers with *style*,' she said.

They split into two squadrons: one covert operation (Pea, Troy and Wuffly) to infiltrate the village for supplies without being seen; and one home team (Clover, Ryan and Tinkerbell) to collect firewood and set up all the shiny PIE equipment.

Pea bought bread rolls, and extra torch batteries, and marshmallows to toast over their fire. Then Agent Troy cleverly remembered to go back and buy matches, so they'd actually be able to light it. It took the very last of the Clem money, but Pea was sure it was exactly what he would want them to spend it on.

Back at the camp, a healthy stack of firewood had been gathered, ready for when it got dark. Wuffly chased invisible rabbits. Ryan scanned the landscape with the EMF detector, video camera at his side, poised to record. Troy and Tinkerbell invented a new special handshake, just for Thrilling PIE members. Clover sat on a blanket with Pea, combing knots out of Pea's hair and humming. Pea tried to write more of *Spookadoo Hall* in her owl notebook, but her mind was flitting about too much for a story that went in a straight line, so she wrote a sort of accidental poem instead.

I smell lavender/grass/sweaty dog/poo/
 fresh air
I hear birds/barking/laughing/humming
I taste imaginary marshmallows I haven't
 eaten yet but will in a bit
I see clouds/a castle/tiny dot people far
 away/a rabbit/two rabbits
I feel Clover pulling my hair/my pencil in my
 hand/happy

By the time she'd finished, the sky had taken on a new quality: still light, but the sun was going down.

Below them, in the valley, the castle fell quiet, the tourists all locked out for another day.

There it was again: that magical thrill in the air, like Blyton fumes.

'Time to light the campfire,' whispered Pea.

Wuffly was sent to lie down inside the yellow tent, safely out of the way. Clover stacked three bottles of water nearby, just in case, and matches were only to be touched by the big three, not Tinkerbell or Troy. They piled up firewood – tiny twigs and bits of bark for tinder, then bigger sticks on top – and lit the fire. It took six matches and some scrumpled-up pages from the owl notebook added to the bark to get it going, which they all agreed was very good for a first try. Before long it was blazing away, wafting a wonderful woodsmoky smell around them. Tinkerbell was allowed to stand guard with a long stick, for log-prodding from a safe distance.

It hadn't felt cold, but suddenly, the moment Pea moved too far from the flickery flames, it was freezing.

Tinkerbell fetched Wuffly out of the tent, so she could curl up at her feet to keep warm. They shared out Clover's spare clothes from her suitcase – Troy looked especially funny in her stripy jumper, with the sleeves dangling down to his knees – and they all wrapped up in extra clothes and blankets. Ryan rolled up his trouserleg and took off his splint, noisily undoing the velcro straps. His leg looked skinny next to the other one.

Clover tipped the sausages into the frying pan.

'How do ghosts like their sausages cooked?' said Troy. 'Terri-fried!'

By the time the sausages were ready, it was almost dark. The castle ruins were all lit up, looking even more magical than before.

'Oh, we forgot ketchup,' said Clover sadly as she pressed a sausage into a roll.

'And washing-up liquid,' said Pea, looking at

the black bits all over the frying pan.

'Who cares?' said Tinkerbell, with her mouth full. 'This is perfect.'

Out of nowhere, a faint voice spoke, oddly muffled and croaky.

Tinkerbell grabbed her torch and swung it around in the dark, bouncing shadows off the spindly trees. Suddenly the top of the hill was a scary place to be, in the darkness, with no adults around.

Pea's hand reached for the sticker on her jumper, and she touched it with a fingertip.

The crackly voice burst forth again.

Clutching Wuffly's collar, Tinkerbell crept towards it, and lifted the flap of the Munros' tent.

'Agent Dad calling PIE Away Team – come in please. Over.'

There, tucked into Ryan's backpack, was a walkie-talkie.

'Agent Tinkerbell receiving you!' said Tinkerbell gleefully, grabbing the walkie-talkie and hurrying back to the fire. 'Hello, Max! Um . . . hang on.'

She handed it to Ryan, who grinned.

'Dad reckons mobile phone signals disrupt spirit activity, so he never uses one if he can help it.' He pressed the button on the side. 'Away Team reporting for night duty! We are monitoring. Zero contact so far. Agent Troy has a gob full of sausage so he can't respond. Over.'

Max's laugh came down the walkie-talkie, all crackles.

'Agent Dad is officially jealous. OK, lads, you know the drill. In case of ghost activity, use code word Fandango, repeat, Fandango. Sleep well, guys, nighty-night. Agent Dad over and out.'

'So cool,' said Tinkerbell as Ryan tucked the walkie-talkie away. 'You should text Mum too, Pea, to tell her we're OK. Unless that'll stop us seeing any ghosts?'

Ryan shook his head.

Pea fetched the mobile phone from her pocket, and typed:

> Having brilliant time so don't worry about us, hope you are writing lots, give yourself a sticker if so, love from your Neditor (and the others) xx

A moment later there was a buzz.

'Mum says *Thank you! Writing loads. Kisses to all of you too! xxxxx*,' Pea read out loud.

It was now so dark that when the phone screen blinked out, she could barely see her own hand. There was just the firelight, and the glow from the castle down below, now shrouded in an eerie mist.

'Marshmallows!' yelled Tinkerbell.

She and Troy took the torch, and hunted out long thin sticks to toast them on.

Before long the woodsmoky smell was joined by a delicious toasty marshmallow smell. Every now and then one caught fire and turned crusty and black, but Ryan said those were the best ones.

They ate the whole bagful.

'Ghost stories!' yelled Tinkerbell. 'I'll start. Once.'

'Upon,' said Clover.

'A,' said Pea, nervously peering over her shoulder and hoping it wouldn't get too spooky too fast.

'Time,' said Troy.

'Um,' said Ryan.

'You can't say *um* − just say the next word that would come in the story. Once Upon A Time . . . ?'

'There?' said Ryan.

'Exactly,' said Tinkerbell. 'That's not my next word in the story, I was just talking. Er. Was.'

'A.'

'Huge.'

'Terrifying.'

'Grey Lady.'

'That's two words, Agent Ryan!' said Tinkerbell.

But Ryan was staring off into the distance, his

mouth open.

Pea spun round. She blinked. Then she stumbled to her feet, letting the blanket around her shoulders fall to the ground, and flung her arm out straight at the road beneath the castle.

'Look . . . Look!' she breathed.

Down in the darkness below was a light, moving slowly through the trees as if through a fog. A tall white shape. A woman, in a long white dress, carrying a glowing lamp.

The Grey Lady.

# CHAPTER 19

# THE GREY LADY

Pea's skin prickled all over.

She rubbed her eyes and blinked, but the figure was still there. It was exactly like the video: a woman in wafty white, gliding slowly through the mist.

'Fandango, Fandango!' Troy shouted. 'Tell Dad, quick!'

But Ryan's left hand was skimming the grass, frantically searching. 'The walkie-talkie . . . I can't find it!'

Tinkerbell grabbed the torch and shone it around on the ground, but all it lit up was clumps of grass, fallen crumbs of bread roll, and Wuffly's wagging tail as she ran around.

'Forget it, it's lost,' said Ryan breathlessly. 'Come on. Find the camera, someone, we need to video her! Let's get down there – get closer.'

Pea waited for Tinkerbell to jump up and volunteer – but she was clinging onto Wuffly, and shaking all over with fright. Clover went to her side, sat down, and wrapped one arm round Tinkerbell's shoulder. She too looked utterly spooked.

Pea looked nervously at Ryan, the firelight casting orange shadows across his eager face. 'Are you sure you can . . . ?' she asked. 'Downhill, in the dark?'

'He can on this!' said Troy brightly. He ran between them, hauling the sledge behind him.

Pea frowned. 'Oh no, Troy, I don't think—'

'It'll be fine – look! He just needs to jump on and— Whoa!'

The moment Troy sat on the sledge at the edge of the hill, it began to slide forward. Pea made a grab for the oversized stripy jumper, but it slipped through her fingers, and suddenly the sledge was sliding down the steep slope, picking up speed and carrying Troy off into the darkness. Within a second he was out of sight. All they could hear was a long wailing yell of terror as he bumped and bounced down the hill – then an abrupt yelp. Then silence.

'Did he hit something?' squeaked Clover.

Pea peered down into the dark, but she could see nothing – only the pale figure of the ghost far down among the trees beyond.

'Troy? *Troy?*' shouted Ryan.

There was no answer.

'What do we do?' whispered Pea, looking desperately round for help – but Clover and Tinkerbell were still clinging to each other by the fire, looking back at her as if *she* must know. Ryan had already dropped to the ground and begun to shuffle down the hill on his bottom, still yelling Troy's name. He was swallowed up by the darkness in an instant. 'Um. OK,' she said, in a trembly voice. 'Ryan, wait for me! Clover, you stay and look after Tink. And, see if you can find the walkie-talkie. Here, give me a torch.'

She took Tinkerbell's. She wanted to ask Wuffly to come too – it would be much less scary in the dark with company – but Tinkerbell's arms were locked tightly around her neck.

Tinkerbell needed Wuffly more, she told herself. Ryan was brave enough to go down there alone in the dark. And Pea had been the big sister all holiday. She could be the big sister again now. She would be fine, and brave, and Troy would be fine too; it was all going to be fine.

Pea struck out, following the fading sounds of Ryan's yells.

The hill seemed even steeper going down than it had coming up, and she slipped and stumbled as she hurried after him. He glanced up as she caught up with him, a flash of panic in his eyes. He was a big brother too, she remembered, and she imagined it was Tinkerbell out there lost in the dark, and felt quite sick with fear – but Ryan whispered, 'Come on,' and they hurried down together, her on her feet, him on the ground, both calling Troy's name.

The juddery torchlight threw huge, weird shadows off everything. Trees became witches, their claws reaching out to snatch her. A scurrying rabbit was a monster, leaping to block the path or trip her up. And below them she could still see that eerie white figure, hovering about in the mist. She seemed to be moving back and forth along the same path, appearing and disappearing behind the silhouettes of the trees.

If Troy was hurt, they would have to cross that path to reach the village and fetch help.

She might have to *walk right through the ghost*.

The torch quivering in her hand, she took a deep breath and kept going.

Eventually she could hear soft, regular breathing off to her right.

'Troy?' Ryan hissed into the darkness, as Pea

swung the torch in a wide arc. 'It's Pea. Troy, where are you?'

The torchlight glinted off the metal runners of the sledge – on its side, wedged in a patch of brambles.

Ryan scrambled towards it, and Pea's torch found Troy sitting up, looking slightly confused.

Ryan grabbed his elbow and gave him a little shake. 'Are you OK? Troy, are you hurt?'

Troy blinked slowly. 'I don't think so. Look, Ryan, I broke my glasses.'

He held up the two halves. The frame had snapped right in half, across the nose-piece, and one of the lenses had fallen out. Pea tried hunting through the brambles for it, but soon gave up.

'Can you walk?' she asked – but Troy just kept blinking, and he began to shiver all over, as if the shock of coming off the sledge had suddenly caught up with him. The wind lifted, rustling through the trees. The ghostly figure still glowed on the path down below.

Ryan's eyes were bright as he gripped Troy's trembling elbow.

'You go,' he said in a choked voice. 'I'll stay with him. You go and get help. And if you get the chance to . . . oh no! The video camera . . .' He stared longingly back up the hill – but there was no time to go back up to fetch it.

'Never mind,' Pea whispered. 'I'll get help. I'll be as quick as I can. Stay here – I'll come back for you.'

'Good luck, Agent Pea,' Ryan whispered.

She began to run towards the path below, her heart thumping in her chest – but in her haste she tripped, and the torch slipped out of her grasp and rolled down the hill ahead of her, sending odd flashes of light all around as it bounced down the wooden steps cut into the hillside. Pea chased after it helplessly, but in the dark she lost her footing.

She put out her hands to stop herself as she fell forward, her momentum carrying her sliding across grit and gravel, bumping her down a few steps. She eventually slid to a stop, panting.

It hurt. A lot. Sharp pain in her hands, grazes on her tummy, on her knees, even on her chin.

She lay still and tried to breathe, and not to cry.

A pair of voices wafted up from the road below. Faint murmurs . . . a man and a woman.

Had someone else come to find the ghost too?

Or did ghosts speak?

Unsteadily, Pea got back on her feet and found the torch, lying a few steps below her. Holding it hurt – there were big chunks of grit stuck in the heels of her hands, with alarming red bits, and her fingers were stiff and swollen – but somehow the pain made her feel braver. The voices pulled her onwards. She limped down off the hillside, across the bridge and onto the road.

There was a car parked up ahead, with its engine running and headlights on. That was the mist, Pea realized, coming from the car's engine running in the cold night; that was the eerie light.

She crept closer, peering out from behind a tree.

The Grey Lady was standing there, right in the middle of the road. White cloth cap, pure white face, holding an old-fashioned lantern.

But she wasn't a ghost at all.

She was just a woman, with white make-up on, and thick coal-black eye shadow on her eyelids.

'I don't know, mate,' she said. 'I didn't mind wandering about in all this rig in the small hours, but I go walking all the way up East Street at this time of night, someone's going to recognize me!'

The man shook his head. 'I told you, I'll pay you extra. Just for this one night, please.'

Pea recognized the voice at once, and gasped out loud.

The man spun round in shock. Fisherman's hat, a fluff of beard around his chin.

Max Munro.

'Hello? Who's that in the . . . ? Pea? You know, you really shouldn't be out and about this late,' he said, in a nervous, over-jolly voice. Then his face fell. 'Are the boys with you? Wait, what have you done to yourself? Did you fall? Are you hurt?'

He reached out a hand, concerned, but Pea ignored it.

'What are you doing?' she asked in a quavery voice, flicking the torch between the two of them. 'Why are you paying a ghost?'

The Grey Lady shuffled her feet, trying to hide her face.

'I know you!' said Pea, recognizing her at last. 'You're Eliza Hood, the archer from the castle!'

'See?' said Eliza, pulling off her cloth cap and wig to reveal her ordinary short hair underneath. 'I told you I'd get recognized!'

Max held up both hands, trying to calm them down. 'Listen, don't panic, OK? I'll sort all this out. Pea's a bright girl – she'll understand. I'm just arranging a little something for my boys, to make sure their holiday's perfect. And Eliza's helping me out with that. Do you see?'

'You mean . . . you paid her? To pretend to be the Grey Lady?'

'Good to know I was convincing in the part,' said Eliza, her smile oddly pink in her too-pale face. 'I should ask for a—'

Somewhere far above, there was a scream – high, frightened, piercingly loud.

Tinkerbell.

'Oh no,' said Max, staring up at the top of the hill and pointing. 'Look!'

Pea stepped out from underneath the trees and gazed upwards.

High above, at the very top of the hillside, a tent was on fire.

# CHAPTER 20

# NOT ON THE TO-DO LIST

The next few minutes were a total blur.

Pea remembered taking the mobile phone out of her pocket, and trying to dial 999. But her fingers were too shaky and swollen – and Max was already on his own phone, saying, 'Fire service,' and, 'I don't *have* a postcode, it's a hill,' and, 'No, I don't know if anyone's trapped inside.'

Pea tried to tug on his arm, to tell him the boys were up there too – his boys as well as her sisters; to tell him it was Ryan and Clover and Tinkerbell and Wuffly, and poor Troy was lost in a bramble with broken glasses – but the words seemed to stick to her throat.

Max's eyes were wild and too close to her face.

The next thing she knew, she was sitting on the edge of the back seat of Max's car, her feet still on the tarmac, and a ghost was trying to make her drink a sip of water.

The fire on the hilltop seemed to be burning bigger and brighter, huge billows of grey smoke drifting down towards the castle.

Pea heard sirens, far away.

She kept remembering Tinkerbell's scream, playing it over and over in her head . . .

All of a sudden there seemed to be a lot of shouty people on the road.

'We've got two kids,' someone yelled. 'Last name Munro?'

There was a lot of commotion, then two clear Scottish voices piping through.

'Put me down! I can walk, you know!'

First Troy and then Ryan were deposited,

wrapped in blankets, on the tarmac near Pea.

'Hello, Pea,' said Troy, pressing one half of his broken glasses to his face like a monocle and squinting.

'Did you see Her? The Grey Lady?' asked Ryan.

'I – I don't . . .' she whispered. Her hands began to shake uncontrollably.

Then she heard a frantic barking, and more shouting, and someone was pulling her out of the car to cling to her tightly, and sob.

'Clover,' Pea breathed into her jumper, clinging back even though it made her hands hurt and Clover stank of smoke – not the nice campfire kind but an awful, frightening burned plastic smell. 'Where's—?'

'Tink's fine, she's fine, she's fine,' whispered Clover.

'I am not!' said Tinkerbell crossly. 'I'm very broken.'

Clover stepped back, and Pea could see

Tinkerbell sitting on the ground, cradling one arm, Wuffly nuzzling her neck. There were tear-tracks through all the smutty dirt on her face, and a little crinkle of misery between her eyebrows.

'What *happened*?' Pea whispered.

'Tink fell,' said Clover, coughing in a horrid, rattly way. 'Wuffly ran after a rabbit, and didn't come back, so Tink chased after her in the dark, and tripped over a rock. I heard her crying so I went to find her. I don't know how it started – maybe the wind blew it, or we left a blanket too close. I don't know. I just turned round and the tent was already . . . ' She waved a hand vaguely up at the fire.

There were people up there now, with fire extinguishers from the pub; Pea could see big puffs of white against the black smoke.

'The video camera,' said Ryan faintly.

'My vintage blue suitcase,' sighed Clover. 'All my clothes . . .'

'Stuff your clothes, what about my arm?' said

Tinkerbell, kicking her on the ankle.

*Molly's tent*, Pea thought dimly. Molly's tent, and the sleeping bags, and the borrowed frying pan – and her owl notebook, with her poem, and her To-Do List . . .

She looked down at her coat, and saw the happy sunshine sticker.

WELL DONE! it said.

She remembered Mum's proud smile as she'd stuck it on. *My favourite Pea in the whole wide world.*

Pea looked at Clover's tear-streaked face, and Tinkerbell's arm, and Ryan coughing, and Troy's broken glasses, and all the worried crowds of people; at the fire engine's blue flashing lights bouncing off the trees, as fire-fighters began to swarm up the hillside.

She peeled the sticker off her coat, scrumpled it into a tiny ball, and put it in her pocket.

There was a new commotion down the road – of voices, and people hurrying out of the way.

And then there was Mum, in her pyjama

bottoms and a raincoat, pencils in her hair and panic in her eyes.

'Hello, Mum!' said Tinkerbell brightly. 'I've got a broken arm and our tent's burned down and it's all Pea's fault. Oh, and Clover's here too because she ran away from Cheese Camp. Sorry. I think we might be being a teeny bit distracting.'

Pea sat on the hospital's waiting-room chair, and tried very hard to think what to say when she next saw Mum.

Clover and Wuffly had gone back to Castle Cottage with Max – mostly, Mum said, so that she could keep pretending that Clover was perfectly busy being Third Banana until her other two horrible offspring were declared well enough to be shouted at. After a nice woman from the pub – a doctor, on holiday – had given them all a poke and a prod, Ryan and Troy had been declared fit, and a taxi had taken Mum, Pea and Tinkerbell to the minor injuries hospital in Swanage. Mum had said soothing, soft things to Tinkerbell, who cried when she moved her arm, while Pea sat silent and scared in the front seat. She'd talked about Pea, when they arrived – date of birth, medical history – while the nurse was deciding if she needed X-rays too (she didn't).

But Mum wouldn't look her in the eye.

Pea couldn't really blame her.

She'd lied about Clover running away.

She'd lied about staying with the Munros.

She was the responsible one, the sensible girl, the Anne – but she'd let their tent burn down, when it wasn't even their tent, and let Tinkerbell get hurt, and scared all those people, and it all could've been so much worse, so very, very much worse, ever so easily.

*I'm sorry* didn't seem enough, though she'd said it a lot. If they gave out stickers that said TERRIBLE JOB! or YOU'RE BAD AND WE HATE YOU, she would have earned them all.

'Look!' Tinkerbell came running down the

corridor, brandishing her right arm before her. It was wrapped in a plaster cast, with hard blue plastic around it. 'It's a greenstick fracture. That means it didn't snap all the way through, just a bit. And I can't go swimming or have a shower for two weeks, OK? 'Cos this bit can't get wet.'

Pea had nothing so dramatic; only a few hurty stitches on one finger for a deep cut, and some cleaned-up grazes with gauze stuck to them.

'OK. Can you have a bath, if you remember to keep your arm sticking out?'

Tinkerbell nodded.

'We'll do that, then. Because you're completely filthy, Stinks.'

Tinkerbell grinned. 'And a biscuit?'

'It's the middle of the night! And you had sausages *and* marshmallows earlier. If you're starving when we get home, you can have some warm milk. But straight to bed after.'

Tinkerbell nodded at once.

Pea looked up, and realized that Mum was watching them both with an odd expression on her face, as if she was noticing something for the very first time.

'I've called us a taxi, girls,' she said stiffly, looking away. 'I'll wait outside. I'll call you when it comes.'

She began to walk towards the hospital doors.

Pea had been very determined not to feel sorry for herself, being left alone while the nurse picked painful bits of grit out of her hands and put in her stitches, so Mum could be with Tinkerbell. But now something in her broke. She stood up.

'Mum,' she said, taking a tentative step forward. 'Mummy?'

Mum set her shoulders at the first, but then she stopped, and turned, and her face went soft and sad.

'Come here, Pea-pod,' she said, and Pea ran into her arms and hugged her very tightly, letting the comforting jasmine-perfumed Mum-smell fill up her nose.

'I'm still very angry with you,' said Mum, through a sniffle.

'I'm still very sorry,' mumbled Pea.

'I've got a greenstick fracture, I need the most hugs,' called Tinkerbell from her chair.

The long taxi ride home turned out to be a very useful thing. This time they all sat together in the back. Tinkerbell fell asleep against Pea's shoulder within minutes, which left lots of quiet catching-up time to talk in the dark.

'Oh dear. How on earth did we end up here, Pea?'

'I don't really know,' said Pea. 'It was all going really well. I was being a good Neditor, and a good Vitória, and I made sure Tinkerbell was having her Famous Five holiday for Clem – everything on my To-Do List . . . but then that got harder, and then Clover came and—'

'Hang on – go back a bit. What list?' said Mum.

She held Pea's sore hand, very gently.

So Pea explained all about the To-Do List, and Dr Paget saying she was the sensible one, and Clem asking her to be the in-charge one, and Mum needing her to be the Neditor one. 'And I thought Clover was fine so I didn't put her on the list – but it turned out she was just pretending so I wouldn't have to worry about her too. I know I should've told you she was here! We all should've. But it didn't seem very Neditorial. And then I had the idea to go camping, so Tinkerbell could have her campfire, and Ryan could look for his ghost, and . . . I didn't think it could go so wrong.'

'Hmm. Well, I quite see that part. And I'm starting to understand the rest, I think. But there's a bit missing. Tell me, Pea, on your To-Do List . . . what did you have to do for yourself?'

Pea frowned. 'Nothing. I had to look after everyone else.'

Mum gave her a look.

'No, I wanted to! I like helping. I know it makes me a boring Anne-type of person, not an exciting George, but it's nice doing things to make other people happy. Isn't it?'

Mum scratched her forehead. 'Well, yes. Being kind and thoughtful; I love that you're those things. But you can't *make* someone else be happy – especially if you're so busy trying that you forget to make yourself happy too. You being my Neditor helped a lot, but you couldn't *make* me ready to write my book. Neither could Special Writing Tea or stickers, or *Ocean Sounds Volume II*. It had to be me, in the end.'

*Blyton fumes*, Pea thought. But Mum hadn't needed those to write her other books. They probably didn't exist at all.

'Who told you that you were a boring Anne-person, anyway? No, wait. I can guess. Tink's wrong, you know. You're not Anne, or George. I don't think any of us are: we're just ourselves – and not even always the best version of that. Mostly I think I'm a better mum than I am a writer – but I don't think I can have been lately. I thought you were on holiday, and all this time you've been working even harder than me.'

Pea shrugged. 'I don't mind. I wanted to come here too. Or – well, I did, until . . .'

Mum shuddered, and stroked Pea's hand. 'Don't. I can't imagine – all of you, camping out there alone – with a fire . . . Oh! We're all going to have a long, horrible talk tomorrow, about things which are fun in a book, but must never, ever happen in real life – yes? And you're going to have no pocket money until you've bought Molly's mum a new tent, and replaced everything else – and you'll write letters to . . . well, I don't even know who to – to everyone in the whole of Corfe Castle village – to say how sorry you are, and to Max for lying to him – and – and . . .'

Pea nodded again and again, till her neck hurt.

'Oh, I'm too sleepy to stay angry,' said Mum. 'I'll be angry again tomorrow. We'll save it till then. But before that I want to know one thing; one very important, very forgotten-about thing. What would your perfect holiday be, Pea-nut? What would you put on the To-Do List, to make you happy?'

Pea thought hard. It didn't take long. Once she had thought of it, she tried to think of something else – something that wouldn't hurt the *Pirate Girls*, or disappoint Tinkerbell – but there was a right answer and it wouldn't go away.

'I'd go home,' she said. 'Back to London, with all of us together. Being on holiday's nice and everything, but actually I like my ordinary life best of all.'

Mum was quiet for a moment. The taxi turned round the last bend, and they could see the ruins of Corfe Castle lit up before them. It was as beautiful as ever, Pea thought, but looking at it made her feel tired.

Pea nudged Tinkerbell awake enough to stumble

out of the car. They stood outside Castle Cottage's red front door, ready to collect Clover.

'You know, Pea?' said Mum. 'I think you're right. I like my ordinary life best of all too. Aren't we lucky?'

# CHAPTER 21

# THE DAY AFTER

When Pea woke up, she could smell smoke.

She sat up with a jolt, but there was nothing on fire; only Wuffly curled up in a bundle of Tinkerbell's unwashed clothes from last night.

Pea tiptoed downstairs stiffly, her hands sore, all her grazes waking up. She found Mum, Clover and Tinkerbell, dressed, sitting at the scrubbed pine table, having a very serious-looking conversation. It was already past eleven o'clock; she had slept right through.

'Are we still in trouble?' she said, lingering in the doorway.

'Loads,' said Tinkerbell cheerfully.

'But I expect we'll survive,' said Mum. 'Now, go and have a wash, Pea. I've arranged for us to go out for lunch.'

Pea thought hungrily of the menu at the pub – chicken Kiev: she could definitely have that again – but when they left, Mum led them across the village square and back to the red front door of Castle Cottage.

'Go on then, knock,' said Mum.

Pea looked anxiously at Tinkerbell and Clover. Everyone had been too shocked and sleepy to talk last night about whose idea the camping plan had been; the thought of being told off by big Max was terrifying. And she couldn't imagine how disappointed Ryan and Troy must be about the Grey Lady.

But Troy opened the door, his broken glasses now taped together across his nose, giddy with smiles.

'Come in! We've got tons to show you!'

Wuffly bounced inside, and they followed her into the living room.

'Afternoon – come in, come, in!' boomed Max. He beckoned cheerfully with a spatula from the kitchen, where he stood at the stove in a too-small stripy blue pinny and his funny little hat.

'Good afternoon,' murmured Pea, confused.

Max buzzed about offering cups of tea and glasses of squash. Pea sank onto the sofa beside Ryan – who looked a little scuffed and worn, but quite breathlessly happy.

'Check it out,' he said. 'We might not have got any shots of her, but someone did.'

He played a new video, taken by someone with remarkably steady hands, of a very familiar-looking Grey Lady. She wafted about through the trees in the mist, eerily lit, just as Pea had seen her from the hilltop, only from a new angle. In fact, Pea thought it must have been taken by someone standing in the road, very close by.

'Incredible, right?' said Ryan. 'And that's not

even the only one! We had three more sent in to the website, by other people who saw her.'

'Two videos *and* a photograph,' said Troy proudly. 'Our website's getting tons of hits.'

The photo was much blurrier. In it, the Grey Lady seemed to be holding onto her skirts, and running away as quickly as she could.

Pea didn't know what to say.

'Hey, Pea? Could you give me a quick hand with the cups here?' said Max.

She tiptoed nervously into the kitchen. 'They don't know?' she whispered. 'Why haven't you told them?'

Max scanned the room, checking no one could hear, then spoke in a low voice, looking deeply embarrassed. 'I meant to – but now I can't bear to. Look how happy they are. I did that.'

An awful thought walked across Pea's mind.

'Did you make it *all* up? The Phantom Squid, and the wee girl in rags you saw on the stairs?'

Max looked aghast. 'Never! I'm a true believer,

a serious investigator. But . . . well, I'm a dad too. Ryan's growing up. He'll be a teenager soon. This might be the last year he wants to join in with PIE and all the rest. I just wanted their summer holiday to be perfect, you know?'

That was the thing, Pea thought, with trying to have Christmas every single day. You had to cheat. Or go camping in secret and burn some tents down and break an arm and some glasses. And that didn't feel perfect at all.

'Will you tell?' Max's eyes were nervous now. 'It doesn't change a thing, you know. That balloon you found . . . Just because that one wasn't a ghost doesn't mean they're not out there. The Grey Lady is too, somewhere. All I did was give her – the idea of her – a little nudge in our direction. But it won't ever happen again, I swear.'

Pea thought about Salty Jake, and Tinkerbell's squashed face when she found out the truth. It had been miserable. But it would've felt worse, the longer she'd kept up the lie.

Pea shook her head slowly and sadly. 'I won't tell. But . . .' She hesitated. 'I know you were trying to be kind, but my mum says you can't *make* people happy – especially not by lying to them. You can't control how other people feel at all, really. Not even yourself. I think mostly you should just listen.'

Max smiled. 'You're a wise little thing, aren't you?'

Pea looked guiltily at the stitches in her sore hands. 'I wasn't yesterday,' she said. 'But I'm doing my best.'

She said a proper sorry to him for the camping plan, and they shook hands: gently but very seriously, as if they were both grown ups.

Then they had a sit-down lunch of posh bacon sandwiches, with fresh grilled tomatoes, fancy herby bread, and lots of tea and squash.

Tinkerbell went upstairs to film a new PIE video for the website – but Pea decided to stay downstairs, and sat in a quiet corner with her book.

Then Mum called them all together.

'Well, I think we all owe Max and Ryan and Troy a great big thank you as well as an apology, don't we, my chicks? That was quite the most delicious bacon sandwich I've ever eaten. But now it's time for us to say goodbye. A proper goodbye, I mean. We're going home.'

'Home?' said Pea. 'You mean—?'

'*Home*,' said Mum. 'It's been a wonderful holiday, and a terrifying one, and I think it's time it ended. Back to London for all of us. Although . . .' She looked at Clover, as if waiting for an answer to a question.

Clover lifted her chin, and nodded. 'I've decided. I'm going to go back to Cheseman Hall.'

'But you hate it there!' said Tinkerbell. 'You ran away!'

'I know. But – well, I do still want to be an actor. If I'm not as good at tap or jazz or sword-fighting as all the little Pawns, then I need as many lessons as possible. So I'm going to go back, and ignore the mean people, and if I catch up even a little bit, then it'll be worth every bowl of horrid soup.'

Troy jumped up from the table and handed her a smoky, muddy bundle. It was her stripy jumper, or what was left of it. 'Sorry about all the holes – it went in some brambles. Did *all* your other clothes get burned?'

'Oh yes. But we're going to stop off at a charity shop on the way back, aren't we, Mum? I'll be the most vintagey actor Cheese Camp has ever seen!'

Mum smiled, and kissed Clover's cheek.

They said their farewells.

They'd barely made it to the village square before they heard a shout.

They ran back, to find Ryan and Troy waiting on the corner.

'For you,' said Ryan, holding out his left hand. Looped on his fingers were three bright green plastic bracelets: PIE identity tags.

'Honorary members only, of course,' he said, giving them a wink over the top of his sunglasses.

'Since you don't live in Edinburgh,' Troy added.

Tinkerbell put hers on at once. Pea bit her lip, then put hers in her pocket.

'Agent Tinkerbell, Agent Pea, Agent Billybob? Good luck.'

'And good hunting!' said Troy.

Troy and Tinkerbell did their new, extra-complicated handshake.

The sisters saluted back, until the boys were out of sight.

'Erm . . . Agent Billybob?' said Mum.

'Don't ask,' said Clover weakly.

'Mum?' said Tinkerbell. 'If I can't have an iPad, can I have a black hoodie and some extra-dark sunglasses?'

'Of course you can, Tink. Just as soon as you've saved up enough pocket money to pay me back for a new tent, and sleeping bags, and lost cushions, and . . .'

# CHAPTER 22

# A DIFFERENT SORT OF HOLIDAY

The rest of the summer holidays were not spent in Corfe Castle village, or camping in the Lake District. They were spent back home in London, behind their raspberry-red front door. And while it was definitely still the holidays, there was a new routine in place.

Mum spent her days next door, sharing a home office with Dr Skidelsky, (who proved surprisingly receptive to motivational stickers, and produced at least twenty pages of her important serious book a day in return for a cheerful swan in a hat, or a pizza slice that said WOOHOO!)

Pea, Tinkerbell and the two Sams were tasked with providing food, drink and comforting neck massages for the hard-working writers next door. Each meal earned more money off the burned-tent debt. So did walking Wuffly and Surprise the puppy, and tidying up, and performing 'entertainments' – small playlets, usually about ghosts, or pirates, or ghostly pirates – sometimes with accompaniment from Clover, warbling lustily down the mobile phone.

The rest of the time, they were under instruction to be as on holiday as possible.

Tinkerbell invented PIL (Paranormal Investigations London), which had a purple logo shaped like a castle, and its own special secret handshake – involving barking, handstands and eating a square of chocolate at the end. She and Sam Two practised it a lot.

Pea read books, and worked on a new comic with Sam One – which they agreed would contain no horses or ghosts. Mostly she wrote letters in her new aquarium notebook.

Dear Ryan and Troy,

Tink says there are no ghosts in Kensal Rise so far, but we have only just started looking and we haven't got iPads.

Mum says there's a poltergeist that eats socks, one half of a pair at a time, but I think she is joking. If not, please advise.

From Agents Pea and Tink

Dear Enid Blyton,

I've thought about this a lot, and I think I've decided that liking you is completely allowed, and so is not liking you, and sometimes I might do both at once.

I asked Clem about the dolls in the shop and he said he didn't like them, either. We wrote them a letter to let them know.

I'm sad I didn't get to meet your ghost. But I'm glad I read your books. Thank you for giving me and Tinkerbell a thing to share (even if she is more interested in paranormal investigations now).

Also it would have been better to mention more fire safety in your books if you have children going camping, because sometimes tents catch fire when you aren't looking.

Love from Pea xx

Dear Anne,

I'm sorry I thought mean things about you, I know you're boring in the books, but probably you aren't in real life. It's just the writer didn't know all the things about you that were interesting.

I've asked Mum to call one of her pirate girls Anne so everyone knows Annes can be brilliant even if they also do the washing-up, boil eggs, etc.

Love from Pea xx

On the very last Saturday of the holidays, their doorbell rang three times in a row.

First came Clover, wearing a *very* vintage outfit of an old wedding dress, a knitted poncho and wellies, and clutching all her possessions in a bin bag.

'I'm here! Hello!' she sang, sweeping Pea into a dancing hold and waltzing her down the hall. 'Oh, I can't believe I have to wait until next summer to go back!'

On her return, Clover's fellow Pawns had been most taken with her brave adventures and tales of running away. It turned out all the Pawns were utterly fed up with having to be bowls of fruit while the Kings and Queens got all the very best parts in *Peter Pan* too – so, led by Clover, they had staged their own production in secret. There had been no Dangling. There was only one Lost Boy. They didn't get to perform it in front of an audience of important starry people. But it had been much more fun than all the Chin Acting – and at the end Candace, the teacher, had taken Clover aside and told her she had 'a clear talent for direction'.

'So I don't need to change my name after all!' said Clover happily. 'No one minds if a director is called Clover Llewellyn.'

The second ring of the doorbell brought the

Paget-Skidelskys. Dr Paget held a raw chicken. Dr Skidelsky carried a barbecue. Sam One had piles of whole sweetcorn, Sam Two had bread rolls, and Surprise was carrying a big box of matches in his teeth.

'I don't think we're allowed barbecues,' said Pea, nervously eyeing the matches.

'Oh, I think we are today,' said Dr Paget, a twinkle in her eye. 'Look who I've got!'

They all shuffled back, to reveal Mum standing behind them, clutching a thick printed wad of paper.

'Is that . . . ?' whispered Pea.

'*Pirate Girls!*' cried Mum triumphantly. 'It's finished! Well, until I send it to the Dreaditor and she tells me all the bits that need fixing – but it's finished enough for me. And as long as only the grown-ups do any of the bits involving fire, we are definitely allowed a barbecue. Oh, Clover, my swan, you're back!'

They all hurried out into the garden to start the

barbecue – so the third arrival had to ring the bell six times to be heard.

'Room for one more?' bellowed a warm fuzzy voice at the end of the hall.

'Dad!' yelled Tinkerbell.

There he was. Clem: not at the end of a Skype call or a letter, but right there on their doorstep, in a pale pink T-shirt and jeans. He looked much thinner than usual, and there were more grey bits in his hair, but he still had his broad daft smile.

'Hiya, babes,' he said, swinging Tinkerbell up into his arms, though it made him groan. 'How's this poor arm of yours doing?'

'All mended!' said Tinkerbell, punching him on the chin to prove it.

'Oh yeah, that'll help my recuperation,' said Clem, dropping her again. Then he saw Pea, and gave her a wonky smile, half fond, half serious.

'Sorry about Tink's arm,' she said feebly.

'Forgiven. Sorry about asking you to be me,' he said, sighing as he gave her a hug.

'Forgiven,' said Pea, wrapping her arms around his pink T-shirt. 'I'm so glad you're better.'

They ate burgers, and sticky chicken pieces, and sweetcorn wrapped up in foil so it wouldn't go too black. Sam One lay on the grass, holding his tummy and groaning happily. Sam Two and Tinkerbell taught everyone the PIL special secret handshake. (Clem's handstands were especially dramatic.)

Then the Paget-Skidelskys had to go home.

They waved them goodbye, then flopped back into their deckchairs. No one wanted to tidy up yet.

'I think this might be my favourite summer holiday ever,' said Tinkerbell, licking barbecue sauce off her chin. 'It's like we've had about five of them, all squished together.'

'Best Thing, Worst Thing!' shouted Mum. 'Quick!'

Clover looked dreamy. 'Best Thing: I made much nicer friends this summer than Agata. Worst

Thing: I have to go back to wearing school uniform next week, and it's going to feel awfully dull.'

'Best Thing: being with my favourite girls,' said Clem. 'Worst Thing: my lungs still feel a bit like someone's got at them with a vacuum cleaner. Tink?'

'Best Thing: Dad's here. Worst Thing: Dad's here and he pinched the last sweetcorn before I could like a big meanie pig.'

'Charming!' said Mum. 'Hmm, let me think. Best Thing: my book's finished! Worst Thing: my book's finished. I know I've made a bit of a fuss about writing it, but . . . well, I miss it already.'

Pea was last to choose.

'Worst Thing: I bet I end up doing all the washing-up,' she said. 'And my Best Thing is . . .'

Pea looked at Clover in her wedding dress and wellies, twirling Wuffly in a dance. She looked at Clem, making bunny ears out of the sweetcorn husks; at Tinkerbell sticking her tongue out; at

Mum, laughing so hard her eyes were squeezed tightly shut. She thought about the *Pirate Girls* book on the kitchen table, waiting to be read, and all the books Mum would write after it.

She smiled.

'My Best Thing hasn't happened yet,' she said.

## THE END

Hi, my name is Agent Ryan Munro of PIE (which means Paranormal Investigations Edinburgh) and I am eleven years old. Susie (who wrote this book) thought it might be a good idea if I told you about the condition I have called hemiplegia. When we met Pea and Tinkerbell for the first time, they noticed that I wear a rubbery, fingerless glove (splint) on my right hand, the fingers on my right hand are smaller and curled up and that I walk with a limp.

My dad says that just before I was born, my brain got hurt and this stopped my right side working as well as my left side. It doesn't mean that I can't do the same things as you, it just may be a bit harder for me and I might take longer. You know the bit in the book where we climb up the hill at night and I fall over a few times? That's because I find it hard to balance. Sometimes I need help to do things. At school my friends always do up my tie after PE. Plus there are lots of clever things to make tasks easier for me, like my elastic shoelaces, or my school sticky mat (so the paper doesn't move around when I'm writing). I usually find my own way of doing things too, like playing on my Xbox with one hand, or getting down that big hill on my bum!

I suppose I have to admit that I can get stroppy at times, but it's just because I get tired more easily. It's also because I get fed up with being different. Wouldn't you get annoyed if your right arm either just hung there or randomly decided to float up? Oh yes, and I totally hate maths! The numbers just seem to move around on the page so I'm not very good at it. But other people with hemiplegia might find different things easy or hard.

Anyway, I have to go now because me and Dad and Troy are hunting the Ghost Bagpiper of Niddry Street. But you can see other children with hemiplegia and hear what they have to say about it here:

www.**hemihelp**.org.uk

**Hemiplegia** is a condition, the effects of which are similar to a stroke. It is caused by damage to the brain (most often before or around the time of birth) and it results in a varying degree of weakness and lack of control on one side of the body. Approximately half the children have additional diagnoses such as epilepsy, visual impairment, speech difficulties, learning difficulties, emotional and behavioural problems. Hemiplegia affects one child in 1000.

HemiHelp is the UK's national charity that provides information, support and events for children and young people with hemiplegia, their families and the professionals who support them. For more information please call 0207 609 8507 or visit www.hemihelp.org.uk

For Children and Young People with Hemiplegia

# A NOTE FROM
# SUSIE DAY

For those who wonder about these things – yes, Corfe Castle is a real place in Dorset. My grandfather was once the headteacher of the primary school there; one summer, he taught Enid Blyton's children to sail in Swanage Bay while she was busy writing, and my grandmother corresponded with her about their shared interest in education. I grew up in a house full of her books. They are what made me a reader. I think I've been unknowingly getting ready to write this book all my life.

Thank you to all the family for helping with

my 'research' via waspy Tea Room scones and sandcastles: to Tina for borrowed Blyton fumes and Best Thing, Worst Thing; to Nicky, entrusting me with a chunk of the family Blyton at the perfect moment; to Jess, James, Rachel and Matthew for 'Bravery' at Dancing Ledge and one hundred other things; to my mum and dad for the house full of books. Many thanks also to Pita, Jo, Sally and Beth who put up with Despicable Me; to the unfailingly reassuring Sisterhood; to Sarah, Ruth, Caroline and Josie; to LH Johnson, who nudged Anne out of the shadows for me, and Jim Dean for unflagging support; and to Charlbury School's Lunchboox group for Billybob.

My immense gratitude to Amy Couture and Neelam Dongha from HemiHelp, and especially to Joanna Sholem and to Rosalyn Burbidge and family, for being so generous with their time and so thoughtful with their feedback. Many thanks also to the HemiHelp Facebook group for all their kind, valuable words.

And for this book and all the rest, thank you to Ruth Knowles and Annie Eaton; to Jess Clarke; to Clare, Lisa, Harriet, Alex and Charlotte, and to Caroline Walsh, for taking such very good care of Pea, and me. You all get a sticker.

Have you read all the Pea Books?

If you enjoyed Pea, you'll LOVE
these fabulously fun stories!